Born to the Land

BORN TO THE LAND

An American Portrait

Brent Ashabranner

Photographs by Paul Conklin

G.P. Putnam's Sons • New York

Frontispiece: Deming today. The Florida Mountains are in the background.

First impression

Designed by Joy Taylor

Library of Congress Cataloging-in-Publication Data
Ashabranner, Brent K., 1921–
    Born to the land.
    Bibliography: p.
    1. Ranch life—New Mexico—Luna County.
2. Agriculture—New Mexico—Luna County.
3. Luna County (N.M.)—Rural conditions. I. Title.
F802.L9A82 1989   978.9′009734   88–26414
ISBN 0–399–21716–9

For Jo Carr

CONTENTS

Born to the Land

UP AGAINST THE EDGE

At the entrance to the Nunn ranch

THE Nunn ranch is in Luna County, New Mexico, seventeen miles north of Deming, the county seat. As we drove to the ranch on a Friday evening in August, lightning flickered on the horizon; dark clouds hid the Black Range to the north, but not a drop of rain hit our car's windshield. Paul and I had visited the Nunns several times in a year of collecting material for this book, and I thought we were accustomed to the arid, semidesert conditions. But the sea of brown, lifeless tobosa grass that we drove through today was almost frightening.

We arrived at the ranch house just as Joe Bill Nunn came in, begrimed and bone-weary from a day of branding. Joe Bill's wife, Lauren, brought iced tea for everyone, and Joe Bill talked about the specter of drought that was beginning to haunt him.

"We're up against the edge," he said. "We've been playing our cards all summer, and we're down to the last one. We're going to have to sell the whole herd if it doesn't rain soon. We've gambled to the point where there's nothing left for the cattle to eat. That old grass out there is black. There's no nutrition in the stems."

Even as we talked lightning continued to flicker on both horizons—tantalizingly.

"It will be heartbreaking to have to sell our breeding herd," Joe Bill said. "We've got them bred up to where they're good producers."

Drought is the scourge of ranchers; there is nothing they fear as much: not poison weeds, disease, predators, or poor market conditions. We knew from earlier conversations that the Nunns had been forced to sell their entire herd two or three times in the past because of drought. And a rancher without cattle is not a rancher at all.

"We can always go to town and wash dishes at the Pizza Hut," Lauren said.

Joe Bill looked out the window at the lightning. "Later," he said, "when it rains and there is grass again and you get back in the cattle business, all you can find to buy are someone else's rejects. And they cost a lot more than the cattle you were forced to sell."

"When it rains hard I'm so happy I cry," Lauren said. "Afterwards we can hear frogs over there in the greenweed ditch, and it's the sweetest music there is. Joe Bill used to play there after a rain when he was a boy, and he gave it that name. After a good rain we just jump in the pickup and splash around the ranch."

That night a shower cooled the air and drummed on the tin roof of the bunkhouse where we were staying. We—inexperienced rain observers—were encouraged. But the next morning when we were at the corral, Joe Bill dug at the dirt with the toe of his boot and showed us that half an inch down the ground was as dry as ever.

"That rain was nothing at all," he said. "There wasn't enough to nourish the roots of the grass."

Sunday night a real storm burst over that part of Luna County and moved as far south as Deming. The streets of the town ran full, and small lakes accumulated under the railroad underpasses. Lightning bombarded the landscape.

The next morning over breakfast Joe Bill looked pleased as he reported two inches of water in his rain gauge. "It was a good soaking rain," he said. "It all went in the ground. This will buy us more time." But he sounded a note of caution about being too exuberant.

4

Smokey and Joe Bill

"That's all it does—buy us some time. If it hasn't rained a lot more by the end of September, it will be too late for winter pasture."

Smokey Nunn, Joe Bill's father, joined us for coffee. Smokey prefers that name to his real name, Ed. He and his wife, Eunice Dean, have a house about half a mile away, and father and son run the ranch as a joint operation, although they own their land separately. Like the rest of us, Smokey was in a good mood.

"When you've just about given up in this old country it rains," he said, choosing to forget the years when the rain had not come at all. He thought a moment and then said, "The last good rain we had was June 6."

I had been impressed on earlier visits by the ability of ranchers

Harvesting cotton. Despite poor market prices, cotton is still the number one crop in Luna County.

and farmers to recall the precise day of a rain. Ask a city person when it rained last, and he almost certainly won't be able to tell you. Ask a rancher or farmer—at least in this part of the Southwest—and he very likely will tell you not only the month but the exact day of the month and probably the time of day the rain started.

Lightning the night before had knocked out the phones on the Nunn ranch, and Smokey and Joe Bill were going to have to ride maybe twenty miles of line—they have to make their own repairs—to find out what was wrong. Even that extra work couldn't dampen their spirits.

It had rained. Today that was all that mattered.

Later that morning Paul and I went to see Frank and Fannie Smyer—friends from previous visits—who have a farm east of Deming. The same rain that elated Joe Bill and Smokey caused some draws to flood and run through the Smyers' place, complicating Frank's preparation of a field for planting wheat.

He told us that on June 13—again that precision in remembering weather dates—hail had hit just as his chiles were beginning to bud.

"Biggest hail I've ever seen," Frank said. "Must have been at least three-fourths of an inch. It was like someone had taken a sword and cut the tops right off of those chiles." Frank looked out over the field, remembering. "Ruined my cotton, too."

But Frank does not take defeat easily. If he did, he wouldn't be in the farming business. He consulted a soil laboratory and then gave his fields a massive injection of iron, magnesium, boron, and calcium.

"It's a new technique, sort of like intravenous feeding," he said. "And, you know, it looks like I'm going to get a chile crop after all.

"With my insurance I broke even on the cotton. But I sure didn't make anything. Something—bugs, weather, the market—will go wrong every year. I feel lucky if we can bring in one good crop a year."

In Deming that afternoon, Paul and I sat across the desk from John Burris and listened to some hard economic facts about agri-

Harvesting chile near Deming. More acres of chile are grown in New Mexico than in the rest of the United States combined. A chile picker averages about $35 per day.

culture in Luna County, where Burris is county executive director for the Department of Agriculture.

"Cattle and crops are the economic mainstays here," he said, "but some of the traditional crops aren't paying the bill. Take cotton. Right now the all-in cost of growing an acre of cotton is between $450 and $500. The probable yield per acre is 750 pounds. The current price of cotton is seventy cents a pound, so you gross maybe $525 an acre." Burris was quiet a moment, then said again, "Won't pay the bills. Grain-sorghum won't either.

"So farmers are going to other things. They can make money on chiles, and they're just starting onions and lettuce. But they can lose on any crop. So many things can affect a farmer and whether his crop will make money. Insects. Cold spring nights can keep a crop from sprouting. Water costs are getting out of hand. There's no dryland farming in Luna County. All the water comes from wells, and it can cost $200 or more an acre to pump water now. Electricity is that high."

"What does the future look like?" I asked.

Burris looked glum. He handed me some reports and statistical charts. "Read those," he said.

FOOD production and food processing in America today are big business. Giant corporations such as Del Monte, Libby's, and Stokeley-Van Camp are prospering in agriculture, but family farms and ranches are disappearing rapidly. The picture is bleak. Between 1983 and 1988 population declined in more than half of the rural counties in the United States. The number of American farms has shrunk from 6 million to 2.5 million since World War II. For the first time since the Great Depression of the 1930s, ranchers are going out of business or declaring bankruptcy. High prices of energy and fertilizer, unstable market prices, drought, scarcity of labor, and competition from foreign crops and livestock all contribute to the problems of farmers and ranchers today.

How to solve these problems is a subject of intense debate in

Washington, D.C., and in the agricultural states. Some people think they cannot be solved. But experts agree on one thing: trying to make a living by growing crops or raising cattle is a risky business in late twentieth-century America.

Farming and ranching are integral parts of the American fabric, but will family farms and ranches survive in the America of the future? What will farmers and ranchers have to do to survive? Is there, in these people, the desire and strength to survive that will match the tough economic odds?

Those were some of the questions that Paul and I wanted to find answers to. We chose Luna County in New Mexico because both ranching and farming go on there on a large scale and because we had been in that part of the Southwest a number of times working on other books. Luna County is a place with its own traditions, rhythms, problems, and view of the rest of the world. Yet in many ways it might be any part of rural America where the inhabitants depend primarily on agriculture or cattle for their livelihood.

We think we found some of the answers we were looking for. We know that we learned a great deal about people who love the land and whose greatest triumph is to make things grow on it. This book is about some of those people and about some of their neighbors in town who are a part of their lives. But to better understand them and the world they live in today, we must first take a look at the past.

BEGINNINGS

Tracks west. The Southern Pacific Railroad brought pioneer ranchers to south-western New Mexico.

R<small>EMEMBER</small>, boys, nothing on God's earth must stop the United States mail."

Those words of John Butterfield to his stagecoach drivers were on my mind the April morning that Paul and I left El Paso and headed west on Interstate Highway 10 for a spring visit to Deming and Luna County. From El Paso through most of New Mexico, I-10 roughly parallels the famous old Butterfield Trail, and I couldn't help thinking about the differences between traveling the route in 1858, when the first Butterfield stagecoaches began to roll, and in 1987.

The splendid four-lane highway would have us in Deming in two hours, even at the leisurely pace of Paul's driving. A passenger from El Paso on a Butterfield Overland Mail Company stagecoach would have reached Deming in about forty-eight hours—if Deming had existed then, which it didn't. The passenger's stagecoach would lurch day and night over bone-jarring ruts, and the driver would feel lucky to have even those to follow.

Stops would be mainly at Butterfield way stations where horses would be watered or changed for new teams and crews and passengers could take "comfort" breaks. The final destination was San Francisco.

15

Looking at the mountains looming up ahead in the semidesert landscape, I thought of another difference between our travel and that of a Butterfield stagecoach passenger. When Paul and I boarded our plane at National Airport in Washington, D.C., for the flight to El Paso, we—like every other passenger—went through a metal detector to make sure we carried no gun or other weapon. A Butterfield passenger would have been told to bring along a rifle. And he would have been expected to use it if Apaches had swooped down from the Goodsight Hills or had sprung an ambush in Massacre Gap.

I talked to Paul about the changes a century had brought, but he was scanning the countryside, his mind on taking pictures. "I've got to get a shot of those yuccas," he said.

But some things had not changed in a hundred years. The wonderful vistas today were the same ones the Butterfield passenger would have seen: a dramatic silhouette of the Florida Mountains, looking like a gigantic battleship, and to the north the 8,400-foot summit of Cooke's Peak "rising from the plains in bold prominence," as an early traveler had written. Other things had not changed: the pure blue of the desert-mountain sky; the tingling freshness of the air; the yucca stalks shooting up in the desert; the Apache plume and blue and white wild flowers stirring in the wind that seems always to be blowing.

On our first visit to Luna County a year ago, Joe Bill Nunn had shown me where the Butterfield Trail cut across land that was now part of his ranch. It was rough country, and I tried to imagine a stagecoach bouncing across it. John Butterfield's dream had been a big one: a fast, sure southern route to California. He had signed a contract with the government to deliver the mail twice a week over such a route from Tipton, Missouri, to San Francisco and back.

He had to build 165 way stations in the sparsely settled, rugged Southwest. He hired eight hundred men as drivers, station managers, and handlers of the two thousand horses and mules needed along the route. Butterfield guaranteed to make the journey from Tipton to San Francisco in twenty-five days. That meant that the

16

Yuccas

stagecoaches had to average 4.5 miles an hour twenty-four hours a day. The seats inside the coach let down to make beds, and passengers got what sleep they could on them. Although it seems impossible, the Butterfield stagecoaches were almost always successful in keeping to their twenty-five-day schedule. Butterfield was held in awe. Some Indian tribes called him the Great Father of Swift Wagons.

John Butterfield's Overland Mail Company lasted only two and a half years before the Civil War caused cancellation of the mail contract and forced the company to stop operations. But Butterfield's pioneering effort to blaze a trail to California along a southern route was the beginning of westward movement and development in the Southwest that has not ended to this day.

After the Civil War tens of thousands of Eastern emigrants followed Butterfield's route to the West Coast, avoiding the mountains and cold winters of the central and northern overland routes. Some hardy souls abandoned their California quest and stayed in New

Mexico and Arizona. Twenty years after Butterfield's company collapsed, the Southern Pacific Railroad laid its tracks through this rough, dry country.

But American settlers and railroad builders were not the first to occupy this seemingly inhospitable part of the Southwest. From about 950 to 1200 A.D. a mysterious people whom historians call the Mimbres Indians lived along the banks of the Mimbres River, which heads in the Black Range, cuts through Luna County, and empties into an underground basin in Mexico.

These Indians were early agriculturists, residing peacefully in villages and raising beans, corn, and squash. Their skills in making and decorating pottery reached an artistic excellence that most experts feel was unmatched by other Indian tribes in the Southwest. Most of what we know about the Mimbres Indians we have learned from the scenes of their daily life with which they decorated their pots: wedding ceremonies, dancing, hunting, even gambling.

And then they went away, leaving pottery buried in the ground with their dead as the only record of their existence. And that is the mystery. Why did they leave? Where did they go? Archeologists and anthropologists think they may have left because severe climate change brought prolonged drought. Scholars think they may have moved south into Mexico or north to join other Pueblo tribes. But no one really knows what happened. They just went away.

Then other Indians came, a fierce nomadic hunting tribe who found the sparsely inhabited country much to their liking. They were the Apaches, and the rugged mountains of southwestern New Mexico became their stronghold in what was to be the last desperate struggle of the American Indians against white encroachment.

For centuries this land belonged to Spain and then to Mexico, but neither country made any serious effort to develop it or to challenge the Apaches' supremacy. After the Mexican War in 1846, however, much of New Mexico, Arizona, and California became United States territory. The Gadsden Purchase in 1853 transferred a final strip of land in extreme southern New Mexico and Arizona to the United States. One of the reasons for the Gadsden Purchase was

An ancient Mimbres bowl

the United States' desire to acquire a good southern railroad route to California.

Under the leadership of the great chiefs, Geronimo, Mangas Colorado, and Victorio, the Apaches fought stubbornly to stem the tide of white settlement, but in the end they were no match for settlers, railroad, and the chain of army forts that the government built around this part of southwestern New Mexico to protect westward-moving pioneers. Finally, the Apaches were removed to reservations in Arizona and another part of New Mexico. Today only a few Indians live in Luna County, and there is no tribal land or structure.

It was the westering Southern Pacific Railroad and the Atchison, Topeka & Santa Fe Railroad moving south that created Deming in

1881. Where the two railroads met in the desert, a town mushroomed into being almost overnight. Ambitious builders and land developers called the motley collection of tents and shacks Deming, in honor of Mary Anne Deming, the wife of one of the railroad magnates. They were sure that their new town would become a major shipping center.

That did not happen. El Paso, one hundred miles to the east, had too great a head start as a railroad center. But Deming did provide a shipping point for cattle on the newly joined railroads, and with a way to get their livestock to market, ranchers from Texas and other parts of New Mexico began to bring their herds to this border area. It was hard country, but there was grass—and water if you knew where to find it.

Deming took root in the 1880s and 1890s and became a real town. Merchants built stores; churches were organized; a five-room school was put up. By 1885 three doctors were practicing and three lawyers had hung out their shingles. By 1890 the population stood at twelve hundred. Silver, lead, and gold had been discovered in the surrounding mountains even before Deming existed, and now smelters were built on the edge of town. For a while Deming citizens thought that mining would make their town into a big city, but the veins of ore pinched out in only a few years. Cattle, however, did not pinch out. A steady buildup continued until seventy thousand head or more were shipped out of Deming almost every year.

As Paul and I found out early in our trips, we could learn a good deal of Deming history just driving around town. Some of the older streets with names like Gold, Silver, Copper, Iron, and Lead are reminders of the early days when people thought that Deming would become an important mining city.

I was puzzled, however, by the fact that many of Deming's streets which date from the town's earliest days are named for trees: Ash, Birch, Elm, Maple, Spruce, Pine. Such trees couldn't possibly have lined the streets of Deming in those days. Someone—it may have been Bayne Anderson, the Deming High School history teacher— cleared up the mystery for me.

20

"People back then thought of their town as an oasis in the desert," he said. "An oasis has to have trees. Deming didn't have any, so they gave it some through street names."

That was a marvelous bit of street-naming and perhaps a self-fulfilling prophecy. Deming may not be quite an oasis today, but it is a fine town with lots of trees.

Paul and I soon discovered that we also could learn local history by talking to people who had lived it. The past and present are still close together in Luna County. One of our early talks was with George Measday, who much prefers to be called Pete. He lives on one of Deming's tree streets—Hemlock—and his memory stretches back to the town's early days. He was two years old when his family moved from Texas to Deming in 1907.

Pete was eleven in 1916 when the Mexican bandit and revolutionary, Pancho Villa, crossed the border with almost a thousand men and raided the little town of Columbus thirty miles from Deming. Villa's forces also hit Camp Furlong, a U.S. Cavalry base near Columbus. After half a day of fighting, Villa and his ragtag army fled back to Mexico but only after seventeen American civilians and soldiers and 142 Villistas were killed.

"Old Man Frost drove up from Columbus in his Dodge even though he was shot," Pete Measday remembers. "People in Deming went crazy when they got the news. They were afraid Pancho Villa was on his way up here. The Deming men tried to organize lookouts and guards. One of them killed a good friend of mine who was riding horseback out on the edge of town.

"A few of Villa's men were captured around Columbus and brought to Deming. A scaffold was built behind the old jail at Platinum and Pine, and those men were hung. No real trial. It was a farce."

We got Pete on the subject of cattle. "No doubt about it," he told us. "Deming was a cow town before it was anything else. There used to be thousands of cattle penned up north of town, waiting to be shipped out on the railroad. Deming was just a sandy, little wind-blown place then. No paved streets. Lots of times you couldn't see

Pete Measday

across Pine Street. It was mostly the wind, but those cattle stirred up plenty of dust.

"Not anymore. No live cattle are shipped out of here by train now. Trucks do all the hauling. There've been lots of changes. Farmers came in. The Interstate brought motels and travelers."

Pete Measday was silent for a moment, and I'm sure he was looking back across the years. "But I'll tell you one thing. The railroad and ranchers made this place."

RANCH COUNTRY

Elizabeth May

THERE are sixty-four ranches in Luna County today. They blanket the county from the high, rolling pastures around Cooke's Peak in the north, where grass can be good, to the harsh, broken terrain along the Mexican border, where only range-wise cattle with an eye for nutritious weeds can survive. Many of these ranches belong to descendants of the original settlers who drove their herds from Texas to this high, dry southwest part of New Mexico in the closing years of the last century and the early years of this century.

One afternoon Elizabeth Hyatt, Elizabeth May, and Muriel Treadwell met with me at the Luna County Mimbres Museum in Deming and answered my questions about the early days of ranching. All are from families that have ranched in Luna County for several generations.

"The May family came here in 1904," Elizabeth May told me. "My husband, Edgar, was twelve years old then. They came from Mineral Wells, Texas. They drove five hundred head of goats, and they had an old buggy and a chuck wagon. They also had some mules and three old hunting dogs. I think it took them three months. They would go as long as six weeks without seeing anyone. They would carry letters from one place to another little town to mail them for people they did meet."

The Mays drove their goats to a place called Lake Valley just north of Luna County but later began ranching in the Florida Mountains south of Deming so that the May children could go to school in Deming.

"The May family has been ranching in the Floridas ever since," Mrs. May said.

She pronounced the name of the mountains Flo-REE-da, and I had learned on my first day in Deming that you mark yourself as a newcomer if you say Florida as if you were talking about the state. Early Spanish explorers named the mountains Florida, which means flowery, because of the abundance of wild flowers that grew on the slopes. American settlers never changed the Spanish pronunciation, and lovely red, blue, white, and orange spring flowers still grow on the mountainsides.

I asked Mrs. May why the family had left Texas in the first place. She said it was because her husband's father had been in poor health. He thought he would live longer in the dry climate of the high country of New Mexico.

"Did he?" I asked.

"Yes," she said. "He was killed by lightning in 1932."

Mrs. Hyatt introduced herself to me as Elizabeth Hyatt of Cooke's Peak. She married Leedrue Hyatt in 1921, and they lived for fifty years on a ranch at the foot of the mountain that is sometimes called the Matterhorn of the West.

The Hyatt family came to this part of New Mexico from Fredericksburg, Texas, in 1897, after several years in another part of New Mexico. I asked the same question—why did they leave Texas and move farther west?—and Mrs. Hyatt gave me the reason that has motivated pioneers since the days of Davy Crockett.

"They felt fenced in," she said.

In this southwest border country of New Mexico, they were, quite literally, not fenced in. At that time this was open range, public land owned by the government, and there were no fences. Anyone could run cattle on the land if they had water for their herd. Water was the key.

Elizabeth Hyatt holding a photograph of her parents and brothers and sisters. Elizabeth is the baby in the picture.

Muriel Treadwell

"The way they got ranches at that time was to buy a spring," Mrs. Hyatt said. "When my husband's folks came in here, they bought Mule Springs and Burro Springs."

"Who owned the springs? Were there already ranchers here?" I asked, before remembering that the first ranchers came in with the railroads in 1881.

"There were," Mrs. Hyatt said, "and my husband's family would buy up little pieces of patented land when they came up for sale."

Patented land is public land that has been transferred to private ownership under the government's homestead laws. That was the

30

way the early ranches were put together: buy land with a spring on it, homestead some land near it, buy other homesteaded land close by as it came up for sale.

Muriel Treadwell said that a search for better range had brought her grandfather to this part of New Mexico. "I remember him telling one of my uncles that he had never seen such beautiful country in his life," she said, "and I can remember myself when they cut grass for hay over a good part of this area. Grass would be up as high as the saddles on the horses."

Mrs. Treadwell's recollection reminded me of a comment by Pete Measday when he was talking about the early years of this century: "The grass was higher in those days. I can take you out and show you where they used to cut thousands and thousands of bales of hay. This country was killed by overgrazing."

"I think it was drought," Mrs. Treadwell said. "The country has never come back from it."

"Every article you read says that it is the overgrazing," Mrs. May said, "but I have lived here, and I think most ranchers try to protect their country from that."

Ranchers are sensitive to the charge of overgrazing. I recalled Joe Bill Nunn and Zay Clopton, a border rancher, telling me that a "real" rancher will even take care of leased public land the way he does his own, not running too many cattle on it, controlling poison weeds, containing erosion. I remembered Lauren Nunn saying firmly, "The country was not killed by overgrazing. The damage has come from long droughts and cutting the land up into farms, then abandoning them because the water table is too low."

When the three ranch women began to pool their memories of drought, I saw clearly that Joe Bill was right when he said that a rancher fears nothing as much as he does drought. They talked about years of drought in the 1920s, 1930s, and 1950s. Mrs. Hyatt said she and her husband had a government rain gauge on their ranch and that during some of the worst drought the gauge would record two or three inches a year, while average rainfall for the area was nine inches. Mrs. Treadwell recalled that during the drought

Zay and Nancy Clopton and their nine-year-old daughter, Kristin, branding calves. The Cloptons live on a remote Luna County ranch near the Mexican border and do most of the work themselves.

years of the thirties, the government killed thousands of drought-stricken cattle.

"Took them up to Mexican Canyon and shot them," Mrs. May said.

"Did the government pay you anything for the cattle they killed?" I asked.

The women had bitter memories.

"Yes," Mrs. Treadwell said, "but very little."

"Twenty-five dollars a head," Mrs. May said. "Something like that."

"Twelve dollars a head," Mrs. Hyatt said emphatically.

The conversation then turned to the common misconception that, because they have lots of cattle and land, ranchers are all rich.

Jim Hurt on the porch of his ranch house west of Deming. Hurt's father brought his family from El Paso to Deming in 1909 in three horse-drawn wagons, a five-day trip. Hurt punched cattle for a dollar and a half a day during the 1930s, but today the Hurt Cattle Company is one of the biggest ranches in New Mexico.

"It is not a lucrative business," Mrs. Hyatt said, speaking of ranching, "and it is awfully hard work."

Each of the women provided specific details for Mrs. May's general observation. They spoke of being wiped out by drought and poor market conditions, of ranchers having to drive school buses, teach school, and take other kinds of jobs to get through the hardest times and piece out an income barely large enough to survive on.

"We didn't have electricity," Mrs. Treadwell said. "We were fortunate to have water."

"We couldn't have paid for electricity if we had had it," Mrs. Hyatt said.

"We didn't have electricity until 1950," Mrs. May added, "and we didn't get telephone service until 1963 or 1964."

Speaking of ranch work, Mrs. Treadwell said, "The man that owns the ranch does most of the work, and if he has sons they are worked right into it. Even the girls work just as hard as the boys."

Mrs. May said, "In our family there were seven, but the four girls were the older ones, so we did the work mostly until the boys grew up to take over."

Mrs. Hyatt returned to the general misconception about ranchers' prosperity. "I think ranchers have had kind of a bad name about being rich because they do drive big cars," she said. "They like good horses and good cars."

"And good boots and Stetsons," Mrs. Treadwell added.

"But if they bought a pair of good boots, they'd last them ten or fifteen years," Mrs. May said. "They only wore them for nice."

It would be grossly unfair to say that Mrs. Hyatt, Mrs. May, and Mrs. Treadwell were complaining about their lives as ranch women. They had simply been giving me honest answers to my questions about the realities of ranching as they had lived them over several decades. When the talk turned to good things, they all had warm memories of ranch life, and I was sure that not one of them would have wanted another kind of life for herself. They spoke of big families working together to build a ranch. They talked about camping parties with other ranch families on the Mimbres River that

Jean Schultz was born in 1908 in Arkansas and was less than a year old when her father homesteaded land south of Deming. He survived financially by digging and repairing wells for ranchers and farmers. Jean still lives in Deming; for a number of years she has painted and sold pictures, mostly oils, of Luna County scenes.

would last for two or three days (after the work was done, Mrs. May put in), of occasional dances that a number of ranch families would go to.

"There were considerable distances involved," Mrs. Hyatt recalled. "When they went, they stayed all night."

"They slept at someone's ranch overnight?" I asked.

"No," Mrs. Treadwell explained, "they stayed there dancing. About midnight they would have refreshments and coffee, and the ones that could would keep dancing."

I seemed to be particularly dense at this point. "But where did you sleep?" I asked. "Did you bring blankets?"

"No," Mrs. May told me patiently, "we partied all night. The little ones we bundled up on benches. It would be daylight sometimes when we got home."

Fern Chadborn, 77, was raised in Deming, but has lived in Columbus on the Mexican border for sixty years. She and her husband were sheep ranchers many years ago. They were wiped out when a snowstorm hit without warning just after they had sheared all their sheep. Granny Chadborn doesn't remember the year but says, "I remember the day—May 4."

Mrs. Treadwell related these memories of the good things of ranch life to our earlier talk about hardship. "I've heard it said in my family," she said. "We were always poor, but we never knew we were poor. We had a good life, and we never knew we were missing things. People in town had more, but that didn't bother us. We had freedom."

Finally, I asked what important changes they had seen in ranch life since they were young girls.

"You have trailers and pickups now," Mrs. Treadwell said without hesitation, "and you don't have to ride fourteen miles before you start working."

I was a bit startled that she would single this out. "In other words," I said, "you put the horses in the trailer and drive to where the work is, where the cattle are."

Mrs. Treadwell nodded. "That's one of the most important changes," she said.

Brands

A LONG branding session on the Nunn ranch showed me how right Mrs. Treadwell was about the importance of pickup and trailer in ranch work. The branding that day was to be in Bobcat Canyon, fifteen miles from Joe Bill's house. We left the house at 8:30 in the morning in his pickup and were at the Bobcat Canyon branding corral after thirty minutes of bouncing over muddy ranch roads.

The horses to be used in the roundup of cows and their unbranded calves were already at the corral, brought in by another pickup pulling a trailer. The horses were fresh, ready to work. So were Smokey, Joe Bill, his son, Justin, and the three cowboys on the

Joe Bill looking over his horses. The Nunn ranch has only thirteen horses because so much ranch work is done now in pickups. A ranch in the old days would have had many more horses.

ranch payroll. This particular branding job would be done in one day. If, as in early years, they had ridden the horses from the ranch house to Bobcat Canyon and back—three or four hours each way— a one-day operation would have turned into two days, at least. Smokey pointed out that back then, before pickups and trailers, they would have taken a chuck wagon, sleeping gear, and a string of horses and stayed out on the range until all the branding was done.

The crew rode out of Bobcat Canyon for the roundup, and we soon lost sight of them in the rolling pasture beyond the canyon. In an hour or so we saw the cattle coming down a long draw, bawling, fighting, trying to get away, the riders yelling at them, waving hats, moving them expertly toward the branding corral.

A branding session on the Nunn ranch

Vaccinating cattle. The Nunns do much of the necessary veterinary work on the ranch.

Then began the all-day ritual of the calves being roped by the hind feet and dragged to the branding chute. Once there, they are branded, dehorned, vaccinated against black leg and other diseases, and—in the case of male calves—castrated. A blue disinfectant is smeared on where the horns have been cut off, and tags are punched into their ears to keep flies away. These medicated tags are effective for from three to five months.

When the calf is released from the branding chute it staggers away and stands silently in a state of shock. But the bawling of the upset mothers continues as does the roar of the butane heater that fires the branding irons to a white glow. The smell of burning hair fills the air, and the faces and clothes of the men become increasingly blood-spattered.

Fortunately, the recuperative powers of the calves are enormous. Soon they take part in the bawling again; by the time the cowboys "mother them up"—make sure they are reunited with their mothers—they trot back to the pasture on reasonably steady legs.

Branding is no fun for animal or man, but it has to be done. The practice of branding goes back to biblical times as the most reliable method of establishing a person's ownership over animals. Even today cattle get through fences and wander; without a brand there would be no way of knowing to whom they belong. A piece of property that walks around is easily lost. When cattle are sold and shipped, an inspector from the New Mexico Livestock Board makes sure that every animal wears the registered brand of the seller.

The design of a brand is very important. A simple one like Smokey Nunn's Rafter X is good because it is easy to stamp clearly on the calf's hide. Brands of several letters or complicated symbols are not so good because they can be hard to apply and to read. A brand with straight lines like the 4H brand 4H of Luna County rancher Jim Hurt is good because it is easy to put on and easy to read. A brand that is hard to change or disguise is desirable; the Circle Arrow , which has been in the Haas family for more than half a century, is such a brand.

The New Mexico Livestock Board permits only one registered

brand per person; but since brands have been registered for over a hundred years and since several members of a ranching family usually have their own brands, many thousands of brands are registered in the state. Thinking of a good new brand that has not already been registered is difficult. For that reason a good brand, already registered, can be sold today for as much as $2,500.

Much of the history, lore, and tradition of the West is written in cattle brands, and southwestern New Mexico is no exception. Every brand has a story—or many stories—behind it. Mrs. May told me of how Edgar May, while still a boy herding goats in the Florida Mountains, had dreamed of a brand and sketched it in the ground with a stick: /\\/\\ . Years later it became his brand and is still the family brand today.

Marguerite Benedict's father bought the RCross brand R± for her when she was a young girl. Every year after that he branded a heifer calf with the RCross brand. The brand and the cattle became her dowry. When she married Dewey Benedict, she took them with her, and the RCross brand became a Benedict family brand. Years later the Benedicts gave their daughter, Jacki, a brand, the Muleshoe ∩ , and Mrs. Benedict said that Jacki quickly became expert in picking out the best heifers to be branded Muleshoe.

There are so many good brand stories. One of my favorites is about the Tangling Y ⟍⟋. Around the turn of the century a young rancher named Thomas Harrington gave his sweetheart the Tangling Y brand. After they were married, Harrington occasionally branded a calf with the Tangling Y, just as a reminder of their courtship; over the years, Tangling Y-branded cattle increased until they became a large herd. This romantic brand is still used by the Harrington family.

And the Bar Broken Heart brand ♡ . There must be a story there, but I didn't hear it.

Learning to read brands isn't so hard if you have a good teacher. Lauren Nunn helped me and gave me a copy of a marvelous history of brands in Grant, Hidalgo, and Luna counties put out by the Borderbelles. The Borderbelles is an organization of ranch women which is affiliated with the state and national Cowbelles organization.

I quickly learned three basic fundamentals of brand reading. Always read from top to bottom. $\frac{O}{O}$ is O-Bar-O. Always read from left to right. M/A is M Slash A. Always read from outside in. (A) is the Circle A. There are many other things to learn if you are going to be a good brand reader. For example, numbers and letters turned on their sides are "lazy." ∧ is the Lazy 7 brand. ⅋ is the Lazy R. An inverted V is always read as an open A. V∧ is the V Open A brand. Letters with wings are said to be flying. The Flying Y brand ⅄ belonged to Ed Nunn, Sr., Smokey's father.

I took a little test and breezed through such brands as Three Slash Slash 3// , although I called it Three Double Slash; Pitchfork ⊃— ; and Three V 3V , which would have been hard to miss. I even got Quarter Circle Lazy U (⊃ . I missed Diamond Tail ◇ , which I called Kite, but I thought my name was pretty good. And I was completely stumped by the Broken Box brand ⌐⌐ , which looked to me like two staples from a stapling machine.

My worst miss was a brand I called the Two Potato. The actual name is Mashed O Ọ . I should have known better. What rancher would call his brand the Two Potato?

"It's a Way of Life"

JOE BILL was restless all day on Thanksgiving. Not working made him uneasy. Ranching is a seven-days-a-week, ten-hours-a-day job. But the three Nunn ranch cowboys—Bucky McCauley, Roger McMillan, and Wes Peterson—had the day off, and Joe Bill knew that he was expected to stay around the house. So, during the morning while Lauren and their daughter, Tami Jo, were cooking

Thanksgiving dinner, Joe Bill

—fixed two leaking trailer tires

—weighed a bull he wanted to sell

—doctored a sick calf

—fixed a leaky faucet in the cattle yard

—worked on his pickup

—patiently answered our questions.

As we walked around, his pocket knife was constantly in and out of his pants pocket; he cut, scraped, and tightened things on the corral fence, the barn door, the windmill, and anything else his critical eye thought needed fixing.

"There's a hundred little things to do that I just don't have time to do on other days," he said as we followed him around, awed by his energy.

Later in the day we stood near the barn and looked at half a dozen cows culled from the herd the day before. Joe Bill's mind is always working on ranch business. "They're not the kind of cows we want to keep," he said. "If we kept them, we'd have to put more time and money into them than they're worth. They'd take time we should be giving to our more productive cows."

Joe Bill pointed to a cow. "Take that one, for example. She has a dry eye. She may have injured herself on a stick or weed." He kept pointing. "That one is a wheezer. She has a respiratory problem that will just get worse. That one has a bad bag with teats so large that a calf couldn't suck them. The calf would starve. That little cow in the back is just wild. Every time we gather the pasture she tries to run off or run over us. Her temperament is bad. Keeping her is not worth the chance of getting somebody hurt. We don't want hospital bills. The other two have bad teeth."

They would all be gone, Joe Bill said, as soon as he could arrange to sell them.

Also in the corral was a fine young Brahman bull, vigorously unhappy about being penned up. He was a beautiful animal, but Joe Bill planned to sell him. "Cattle buyers are prejudiced against a Brahman-Hereford cross," he said. "They don't have enough hair to keep warm during winter in the Texas feedlots. He's a registered bull. If I have to sell him for slaughter, I'll lose a lot of money, but I might lose more if buyers keep rejecting his calves. We'll try to sell him as a breeding bull to a rancher in another place, maybe Arizona. We'll sell him for meat only as a last resort."

The talk about somebody getting hurt reminded us that the first time we had met Joe Bill a year ago, he was hobbling around the house; the day before his horse had reared and come down on his foot. Paul reminded Joe Bill of that.

"Accidents happen all the time on a ranch," Joe Bill said. "I tell time by the sun when I'm working because I can't wear a watch a week without breaking it. I can't wear a ring either. If you see a rancher with a missing finger, you can be sure he had a ring accident.

"You have to exercise a lot of caution, especially if you are by yourself. If your horse falls and your foot catches in the stirrup, the horse can drag you to death."

Joe Bill told us about a terrible accident that Smokey had right after Joe Bill and Lauren were married. Smokey had his rope on a Brahman calf which turned and ran under Smokey's horse. Smokey was thrown and one leg caught in the rope, making him dangle behind the horse, which was kicking him. Finally, someone cut the rope with a knife, saving Smokey's life.

Once, Joe Bill told us, he was standing behind a gate when a calf kicked it against him, breaking several ribs. "Another time my horse fell on me," he said. "Then it got up and fell on me again."

Lauren had come out to tell us that dinner was ready. "That time we took him to the hospital," she said.

After the Thanksgiving feast Joe Bill was in a mellow mood. He sat around for almost an hour doing nothing before he got up and started again on the hundred little things that needed to be done. Justin, who was seventeen then and a senior at Deming High School, announced that he was going to town to spend the night with friends. Joe Bill reminded him that he would be needed to help drive cattle the next day.

Justin and friends on a Saturday evening in Deming

Joe Bill working cattle

WITH the Thanksgiving day of rest behind him, Joe Bill was ready for an early start Friday morning. The cowboys, Bucky, Roger, and Wes, were on hand, but Justin had not returned from Deming. Joe Bill knew that Lauren had plans to visit a friend that day, but he told her that he really needed her to take Justin's place. Lauren—like every other member of the Nunn clan—is a fine rider. She dressed for a day in the saddle and joined the group.

"That's a lesson ranch wives learn soon enough," Lauren told us. "Work comes first."

The work that day was to drive cattle from an enormous pasture. Paul and I marveled at the immensity of the prairie. The winter grass is dazzling in the sunlight; setting out on it, horsemen look like small boats on a golden sea.

Joe Bill estimated that there would be four hundred head of cattle in the pasture. Riders started at three corners and drove them down toward a corral next to the old house where Smokey and Eunice Dean used to live before they built their new one. It was a slow business. The cattle didn't want to be driven, and the riders were constantly going after breakaways. As soon as they got them back with the main herd, others would run off in another direction. But experience, skill, and patience paid off; inexorably, the cattle were forced toward the corral.

At just the right moment, Eunice Dean appeared in her pickup with a hot meal of roast beef, potatoes, fresh bread, slaw, canned pears, and cookies. Everything was spread out on the tailgate of her truck, and Paul and I—who had not chased a cow or yelled at a runaway calf—ate with the gusto of trail-drive cowboys.

The main purpose of the day's work was to separate calves from cows for weaning. The afternoon was spent in the corral with everyone enveloped in a cloud of dust as calves were separated, cows were vaccinated, and those destined for immediate sale were culled. As during branding, bedlam reigned as cows and calves bellowed nonstop.

THE Nunn family has been ranching in New Mexico for four generations, spanning nearly a hundred years. Smokey and Joe Bill own their land separately and lease some from the U.S. Bureau of Land Management—a total of 130,000 acres. To get his land, Joe Bill has bought up two other ranches, one of them the ranch on which Smokey was born sixty-five years ago. Even by New Mexico standards the ranch is good-sized.

Joe Bill and Smokey own their cattle separately, and each has his own brand. Joe Bill's brand is Lightning Bar ⌐ , Smokey's is Rafter X 𝕏 . Eunice Dean also has her own brand, X Slash T X/T, which she has had since she was a young girl. Joe Bill and Smokey keep separate books and sometimes sell cattle separately. But many parts of the ranching operation they carry out together. They buy supplies together to get better volume prices. They often sell cattle together because buyers want to buy larger quantities. They hire cowboys together. Branding and most of the other ranch work are joint operations.

Smokey and Eunice Dean got into the ranching business in their youth; they did it from scratch, without any family help. Joe Bill and Lauren did the same. Except for the ten-acre plot on which their house is located, they have paid for everything themselves, all the land, all the cattle. The family legacy for both Smokey and Joe Bill was not cash, land, or cattle; it was a deep knowledge of the cattle business that came from working on their parents' ranches from the time they could ride well enough to stay out of the way of a bad-tempered cow. Joe Bill is Smokey and Eunice Dean's only child, and they raised him by strict rules. Joe Bill still regards Smokey as "the boss."

"He's worked hard all his life," Lauren told us, talking about Joe Bill. "He has to be putting out a hundred percent all the time or he's miserable."

According to Lauren, Joe Bill's only relaxation is roping. "Sometimes in the spring and summer he will rope in the evening with three friends who live near here," she said. "He also ropes with Tami Jo sometimes."

Three generations of the Nunn family: Eunice Dean, Smokey, Lauren, Joe Bill,
Tami Jo, Justin

Lauren's grandparents had a small ranch near Deming and later
in the Gila Wilderness, deep in the Black Range. Lauren spent many
summers with them, but otherwise she grew up in Deming with no
ranch background. She and Joe Bill were acquainted from the first
grade, finally focusing on each other in high school.

Joe Bill always knew that he wanted to go to college. "I could see
that in the ranching business you never knew when you were going
to be hurt," he said, "when you would need something else to fall
back on."

Joe Bill majored in agricultural economics at New Mexico State
University, and his straight A average earned him a scholarship.

51

Still, finances were tough. Lauren was Joe Bill's wife by then and also a student, and she remembers their college days as good preparation for the economic hardships of starting a ranch.

"I used to iron his buddies' shirts for ten cents apiece to get us a little extra money," she said.

So impressive was his academic record that, upon graduation, Joe Bill had a number of job offers. But after four years of college and town living, he was ready to return to ranching; and Lauren was ready to learn to be a ranch wife. Together, over most of two decades, they have built a ranch.

Discipline is an important word to Joe Bill. He uses it often. "You've got to have the discipline to do without things—like a piece of equipment—until you can afford them," he said. "For years we did without our stock trailers although we really needed them and they would have made our life a lot easier."

He paused and thought a moment. "Now we need a cat real bad." He was talking about a caterpillar tractor. "But we'll put it off until we're in the right financial shape to buy it."

"When I had two babies I was doing clothes on a washboard," Lauren added. "Then one day we could afford a washing machine."

Joe Bill sees the three keys to successful ranching as weather, the market, and management. There is little that a rancher can do about the weather except try to keep the size of his herd in balance with the supply of grass. There is little he can do about the national and world price of beef except try to calculate the best time to sell. But management is a different story. A rancher can do a great deal about how his ranch is run.

Joe Bill keeps a notebook and a small calculator in his shirt pocket, and throughout the day he is constantly running figures and writing in his notebook. (*Saw a crippled cow in cotton pasture. Fix float valve at adobe well.*) Once Joe Bill left a notebook in his shirt, and it went into the washing machine, washing away a month's notes.

"It wasn't too good on the marriage," Joe Bill said, but he smiled at the memory.

Now Lauren checks all pockets before shirts go into the wash.

There is a larger calculator on Joe Bill's office desk in the house. He uses that as he pores over big yellow legal pads late into the night and often early in the morning. Cash needs for feed supplements, equipment, repairs, wages, and family needs must be balanced against income from cattle sales. When it is time to sell cattle, Joe Bill figures down to the penny what he can afford to sell them for.

Buying cattle is in some ways even harder. "In this business," he says, "you have to make decisions today, and you may have to wait years to find out if they were good decisions. You buy a bull today, and it may be quite a while before you see the calves and you know whether you made a good pick."

Management of a ranch is not something that just happens in an office. The decisions that are made out on the range are just as important, if not more important. Joe Bill made that point clearly one day as we rode around the ranch with him.

"Good management is knowing your cattle," he said. "As you move around you are always observing. You see that that calf over there belongs to that cow with the white spot on its nose. Cows that we keep around for a long time—and some of them are with us twelve years—are individuals. If you've ever had to doctor one, you don't forget it. You remember what kind of calf a cow has. If it was a puny old calf because—say—it didn't have enough milk, you cull that cow out later. Sometimes a cow may be big and pretty, but she has the scrawniest calf. Or a skinny old cow may have fat, healthy calves. You remember those things. Some cows are slow breeders. We cull those, too.

"We check a cow's teeth. If they're worn down, the cow has trouble chewing grass and will have trouble producing enough milk for her calf. Generally we will keep cows ten years before we start checking to see if they have good teeth. If they don't, they become hamburger. We keep track in our head of how old a cow is, although some ranchers will brand a date on them. There are a lot of variables which determine whether or not a cow stays in the herd."

Joe Bill talked about drought, a subject never far from his mind. "During drought we have to cull deeper to try to make sure there

Joe Bill and Lauren. Office work is as much a part of modern ranching as is herding cattle.

will be grass for the healthier cows. If the drought is bad we may have to sell all of them and start over when the drought ends. Before we take that step we try to lease land in other parts of the state where there is more grass and truck them over there. The worst drought in my lifetime was in '56. It actually started in '53. There was no rain until '58. I was a kid, but I'll never forget how barren this land looked.

"It can take years and years to recover if you have to sell your breeding herd. You've spent a lot of years of your life on them. You have to care for them all year long, giving them extra nutrients when they need them, trying to keep them away from poison weeds, moving them around from pasture to pasture for the best grass. You take care of them so they will take care of you. You can't just put them out to pasture and then go get them when you need money. You have to care for them constantly. You have to show them where water is. Otherwise they'll get hung up in a fence corner and die of thirst. Every few days we get a horse and ride pastures just to look them over. During calving season we have to be extra observant."

We stopped at a windmill, and Joe Bill got out of the pickup to have a look at it. There are thirty-five windmills on the Nunn ranch. Each has its own name: the hot well (which taps a hot underground spring), the house well, the adobe well, the cotton well (surrounded by cottonwood trees). Similarly, all of the pastures have names. Joe Bill has a complete map of the ranch in his head.

"We keep a maintenance log on every windmill," Joe Bill said. "Have to make sure they're working—no broken water lines or stuck float valves—because cattle are accustomed to drinking at the same water tanks. In hot weather they dehydrate quickly and can die in three or four days without water."

We drove on, the road here paralleling a fence that seemed to stretch into infinity. "A rancher never runs out of things to do," Joe Bill said. "Take that fence. All our fences—every year—need constant maintenance. In winter wire tightens up. We ride the fences then and we say to ourselves, 'Boy, these fences are in good shape.' Then in the summer the wire loosens and we say, 'Why didn't we fix these things last winter?'"

In this treeless country steel posts are coming into use. They cost $2.50 each. Joe Bill doesn't like them, though, because wire is harder to tighten on steel. Tightening wire is easier on cedar posts, and they are less expensive than steel. But installing cedar posts is harder and more time-consuming because a posthole digger has to be used.

"Look at that old fence," Joe Bill said, pointing to a stretch that was sagging so badly the wire seemed to be holding up the posts instead of the other way around. "Some of those old posts were put in by my grandfather. We're always short on time, so we just keep

No one likes to mend fences, but it has to be done.

patching. And fencing gets awful monotonous, so we put it off as long as we can.

"Ranching is a series of minor crises which you try to catch before they get serious. Every day you find at least one thing—some days a dozen—that has gone wrong. If you're not a good manager these problems will take their toll and at the end of the year you won't have money to pay on your bank note."

That comment was a reminder that Joe Bill, like most ranchers, stays perpetually in debt to a bank.

Joe Bill returned to the subject of calves. "The whole year you've got to be watching them. If you don't take care of them constantly, calves won't weigh as much as they should. You can't afford to cut corners. If you scrimp when you should be feeding, they'll get in poor shape, and it will take them a long time to recover. If they get poor in the winter, it may take them all spring and summer to get back in shape."

Joe Bill's theme was constant vigilance. The fruit of vigilance and lots of hard work would be a good healthy calf.

Back at the house that evening, sipping a glass of Lauren's good iced tea, Paul summed up his feelings. "Ranching is a mighty tough way to make a living."

Joe Bill nodded. "I guess," he said. "But it's not just a way to make a living. It's a way of life. It's a family tradition."

Smokey

PAUL and I drove to the Nunn ranch on the second day of our April visit. Joe Bill had told us before we arrived in Deming that they were having serious trouble with tansy, a poisonous weed of the mustard family. I could see patches of it as we turned off the highway and took the dirt road to the ranch house. The mustard looked beautiful at a distance—feathery yellow heads tossing in the wind reminded me of Wordsworth's daffodils—but I had read about the plant and knew it could be deadly to cattle if they ate much of it.

We were at the corral an hour before sunset when Smokey, Joe Bill, and Justin came in with a load of stricken cattle, four cows and two calves in the gooseneck trailer attached to the pickup. We waved hello but stayed out of the way. Joe Bill let down the trailer gate, and they choused the stumbling cows, blind from the poison, into the corral. The calves followed, terrified.

Finding the poisoned animals and getting them to the corral was just the beginning. Now each one had to be "drenched," which meant forcing water through a tube into the stomach of the struggling beast. This treatment would have to be repeated time after time until all poison was flushed from its system. Tansy poisons the cow's nervous system; the animal loses the ability to drink water, and then it goes blind. Death is inevitable unless it is found soon enough and drenched. Calves are victims, too; they take in the poison through their mother's milk. Recovery, including return of sight, takes two or three weeks.

I watched Smokey as the three men wrestled with the cows and calves. They had to be exhausted, all three of them. They had been combing the range for days, looking for cattle walking blindly in circles or stretched helplessly on the ground and then bringing them in for drenching. At sixty-five, Smokey was twenty-five years older than Joe Bill and forty-seven years older than Justin. He had to be feeling those extra years, yet he worked with the same energy and intensity as his son and grandson.

Looking at Smokey now, I remembered something Joe Bill once said to me about his father: "Smokey wouldn't live six weeks if he retired, if all he had to do was check the post office and watch TV." I studied the concentration on Smokey's face as he held down a calf while Joe Bill worked on it. Joe Bill is right, I thought. Ranch work is as much a part of Smokey's staying alive as breathing and eating.

Smokey

At last there was a break in the work, and Smokey walked over to where I stood. We shook hands and he said, "Welcome back."

"I know you're busy and tired," I said, "but I hope Paul and I can have a talk with you before we leave Deming."

"Come on over tonight," Smokey said and went back to work.

That night when we went to Smokey and Eunice Dean's house we found Smokey rather philosophic about the tansy mustard. "It just blowed in from somewhere about ten years ago," he said. "It's good graze when it first comes up, but it's poisonous for three weeks while it flowers. Locoweed and peavine can cause trouble, too."

Another deadly threat, Smokey said, is nitrate poisoning. If there is a sudden, hard freeze nitrate in the soil can be forced into any weed. "Three or four years ago we had friends west of Deming who lost hundreds of cattle to nitrate poisoning. The nights got real cold without warning, and there was no way to corral all those cattle."

There isn't much that Smokey hasn't seen or doesn't know about ranching, both good and bad. He was born in 1922 and grew up on his father's ranch in the foothills of the Black Range, not many miles from where he and Eunice Dean live now. Smokey's grandfather, David Milton "Greeley" Nunn, came to the Black Range from Missouri around 1890 to make his fortune in ranching. No one now living, not even Smokey, knows how he got the nickname Greeley, but the general belief is that someone gave it to him because he followed the advice of the nineteenth-century journalist Horace Greeley to "Go West, Young Man."

But in the remoteness of the Black Range, even at that late date, Indians were a problem, particularly in cattle theft, and Greeley Nunn gave up and went to work in the silver mines. When that got tiresome, he tried ranching again and never did anything else after that but ranch. He had three sons—Pryor, Emmett, and Edward—all of whom became ranchers. Smokey, Edward's son, is a third-generation Nunn rancher, Joe Bill, of course, fourth generation.

I asked Smokey how he got that nickname. "One of my uncles called me that when I was one day old," he said, "and I've been

Marcos Aldaco has a house on the outskirts of Deming where he takes care of a big vegetable garden and raises goats. Born in 1904, Mr. Aldaco remembers stories his grandfather told of being captured by Indians and being kept by them for twenty years.

Smokey ever since. I think it was because I was born with a lot of black hair."

Smokey thought that he would give college a try and enrolled at New Mexico State University after he finished high school, but World War II began during his freshman year and ended the college notion forever. He wanted to enlist, but instead he was called back to work on the Nunn Brothers ranch, a ranch owned jointly by Pryor, Emmett, and his father, Edward. All of the other young Nunn men were already in the war; three of Smokey's cousins had been captured when Corregidor in the Philippines fell to the Japanese early in the conflict.

Smokey did what he had to do, which was help grow beef for a nation that needed food. One good thing that came out of his brief college stay was that he met Eunice Dean there. She left the university at the end of her freshman year, and she and Smokey were married. They began their life together on the Nunn Brothers ranch working for $40 a month and a place to live. It was a tiny house with no electricity, no icebox. Lamps and stoves were fueled with kerosene.

"When we finally got an old kerosene refrigerator that someone was throwing away, it was like a little bit of heaven," Eunice Dean remembers. But she had come out of a New Mexico ranching family, and no one had to tell her the facts of life.

When Smokey's brother and cousins came back after the war, Smokey and Eunice Dean made a quick decision. "It just seemed to us that we should get off the ranch and let them settle back in," she said.

So they borrowed some money from the bank and bought a piece of land. "We just moved across the highway," Eunice Dean told me.

Very much in the way that early ranches were put together, Smokey and Eunice Dean put theirs together: borrow money, buy a piece of land, lease some land, pay back the money, do it all over again.

The first time we ever talked with Smokey, he said, "I'm still buying the ranch. I've been doing it for years. Every winter after I ship my last cattle I go in and borrow more money. I'm never out of debt."

The last time we saw him, a year and a half later, Smokey was feeling more relaxed. "I'm sixty-five," he told us, "and I'm finally out of debt." And then he added, "Almost."

Joe Bill once talked to us about the difference between his and his father's approach to selling cattle. "He doesn't study the current market and use the calculator the way I do," Joe Bill said. "He relies on his experience and doesn't worry about making a few dollars less. He doesn't try to maximize as much as I do.

Smokey and Eunice Dean in the corner of the garage where he does his painting

"I'm more inclined to hold out for higher prices, but he has seen from experience that holding out can lead to real trouble since the market can go down and you can lose your shirt in the process."

Smokey's only comment on this was about the calculator. "I can figure in my head as fast as he can on that thing," he said.

Like Joe Bill and his roping, Smokey has only one pastime: he paints pictures. I first became aware of this when I noticed that the garage of their house was full of half-finished oil paintings. "He can't put in two consecutive hours," Eunice Dean said, "only when there's a sandstorm. Painting is just pure enjoyment for Smokey. He's never even entered an art show."

"I can't draw a tree or a hill, but I like to paint pictures of horses

63

and action scenes," Smokey told me. "I've been drawing since I was a kid six or seven years old. The margins of my old schoolbooks are filled with drawings of horses. I guess that's why I never learned very much."

About seven years ago Eunice Dean bought Smokey a set of oil paints and a self-instruction book on oil painting. Smokey says that he got through only two lessons, but he has been doing oil painting ever since.

Smokey is a man who is very careful about letting his feelings show and especially about seeming to be sentimental in any way. But occasionally a little bit of how he feels about this hard but beautiful desert-mountain country in which he has spent his whole life shows through.

"They say," he said to us once, "that if you wear out a pair of boots in this country you will never leave."

But then he couldn't resist adding, "Of course, if you stay that long, you won't have enough money to leave."

Young in the Saddle

DURING my conversation with Mrs. Hyatt, Mrs. May, and Mrs. Treadwell about ranching in the past, the talk at one point moved to the subject of ranch children. "These little kids start out riding early," Muriel Treadwell said. "My little boy and girl were riding horses by the time they were three and four. They grow right up in the saddle. They're usually sitting in a saddle by the time they're six months old."

Mrs. May added, "The children had a lot of responsibility, too. They had their livestock to take care of, and they didn't want to do the things that kids do now."

64

Justin

The women then talked about the lack of a sense of responsibility among young people today. But their final conclusion seemed to be that it might be a problem in town but "not in the country."

As I got to know Justin and Tami Jo Nunn, it seemed to me that they were excellent examples of what the women had been talking about. Justin, who was seventeen when I first met him, seemed very much at home in the saddle. My judgment is not expert in such matters, but when he, his father, and the hired cowboys were driving cattle to the branding corral, I thought he held up his end of the work as well as any of them. Later Justin told me that he started to work with cattle as soon as he could ride well enough.

"About the second or third grade," he said.

Tami Jo was sixteen and a junior in high school at the time of our first visit in 1986. Joe Bill says that his daughter is a "natural cowboy" and better on horseback than Justin.

"But Justin is better on the ground," Joe Bill said, meaning at tasks like wrestling a struggling calf into the chute for branding.

Smokey maintains that ranch horses today are not much good because they don't get ridden enough. "They're just something to keep your feet from dragging on the ground," he grumbles.

But Tami Jo has two beautiful horses, Cheyenne and Hatchet, that are a joy to watch when they are working cattle, separating calves from their mothers for branding or weaning. Tami Jo has competed in 4H horse shows and local rodeos since she was in the fourth grade and has won an impressive array of trophies, ribbons, and belt buckles. Her favorite events are the stake race, in which the competitors ride a pattern around two poles at top speed, and the barrel race, which involves doing a cloverleaf pattern around positioned barrels.

She has also done well in keyhole races. In this event the horse and rider enter a keyhole diagram chalked on the ground. Once inside the keyhole, the horse pivots and leaves through the entrance. All this must be done fast and without stepping on the lines of the keyhole diagram. Both Hatchet and Cheyenne are rodeo horses,

Tami Jo getting one of her steers ready for the Southwestern New Mexico State Fair cattle show

though Hatchet has retired from competition since an accident a few years ago. But he still does his share of ranch work.

From the time they both were young children, Justin and Tami Jo have entered steers every year in the Southwestern New Mexico State Fair cattle show held in Deming. One year Justin won the Grand Champion Steer Award, and he has placed first, second, or third every year he has entered. Tami Jo won Reserve Grand Champion one year, and her entries have placed for eight straight years. On the wall above her desk is a crowd of colored ribbons that she has won.

Tami Jo in her room at home. The ribbons on the wall represent winning entries in cattle shows.

Getting an animal ready for the big state fair competition is just plain hard work. Three months at least are needed to get a show calf halterbroken, working with the animal every day. The process is very much like getting a pedigreed dog ready for a show. The steer must perform right when it is paraded before the judges, must respond properly to the person handling it.

The show animal must be brushed every day so that its coat will acquire a rich luster. As show time approaches, Tami Jo and Justin wash their animals and even blow-dry and shape their hair. They sculpt them like a work of art. All of this requires patience and skill that are not easily learned. But the rewards are the satisfaction of doing well in the show and of putting some prize money in their college funds.

Another payoff of all this work—perhaps the most important payoff—is a knowledge of animal quality that Tami Jo and Justin have developed. Usually they select a likely show calf from the Nunn herd, but sometimes they decide to buy one. That was the case last year when Tami Jo bought a calf at auction, and her choice caused something of a row between her and her father. Joe Bill was sitting right behind her at the auction and told her to stop bidding because the calf was inferior. She bought it anyway, trusting her own judgment, and was later vindicated when it developed into a fine animal and won a prize at the state fair.

"It gave me an odd feeling to have her instincts on the calf turn out better than mine," Joe Bill admitted. But he spoke with a touch of fatherly pride.

Lauren says that Justin and Tami Jo were better at preparing their animals when they were little; then they faithfully trained and groomed them every day. By the time they were sophomores, they weren't quite so faithful—too many distractions at school and with friends. Tami Jo is a member of the Deming High School girls' basketball team, the Wildcats. She loves basketball, never misses a Boston Celtics game on television if she can help it.

Justin has a lot of friends in Deming and likes to be with them.

He works hard on the ranch during the summer and on weekends and sometimes after school, but he still manages to go into town frequently in the evenings. Sometimes he spends the night with a friend. And once in a while—like the day after Thanksgiving—his desire to be with his companions gets in the way of his ranch responsibilities. But that does not happen often.

Justin's most prized possession is a yellow pickup given to him by Smokey. It had fifty thousand miles on it when he got it, and he probably has added another twenty-five or thirty in the less than two years he has had it. Most of them have been put on driving the twenty-mile stretch of State Highway 26 that connects the ranch with Deming. Driving the pickup back and forth to school adds about 250 miles a week to the odometer.

"Justin has four bosses," Lauren says, meaning Joe Bill and herself, as well as Smokey and Eunice Dean, Justin's grandparents. "That truck means freedom for him. He just uses it to get away from the ranch."

Justin thinks he wants to go to college; he has no idea what he wants to study, but he does know that it won't have anything to do with ranching. It isn't that he doesn't like ranching. He says that sometimes when he is riding the range, he thinks: this is something I can do really well. This is cool.

Right now, though, he wants to get away, be on his own, try new things, see new places. And then maybe he will turn to ranching, borrow some money, start a little place on his own. But he isn't sure, not yet.

Tami Jo is sure that she would like to be a rancher someday but not before she has gone to college and earned a degree in education. She wants to teach and be a basketball coach before she thinks about anything else.

"Ranching is a way of life," Joe Bill said. "It's a family tradition."

Will Justin or Tami Jo or both of them feel the pull of that tradition the way their father and grandfather felt it? Many things can happen to their life directions once they get away from the ranch. But as you watch Tami Jo so much at home in the saddle or Justin so confident in the midst of a chaotic branding session, you think you know the answer to that question. And you think it is yes.

FARM COUNTRY

Reminder of the past on the original Smyer homestead: old wooden wagon wheels that were once part of an ore wagon belonging to Frank's grandfather

AT Pete Measday's house I saw among his keepsakes an article about the country around Deming taken from an early 1900s copy of the *El Paso Morning Times*. The article spoke glowingly of the Mimbres River Valley being converted from a desert into "one of the richest agricultural sections of the Great Southwest." According to the article early settlers who arrived by prairie schooners in the 1880s began to drill wells and discovered the "lost river" which made the valley "bloom like a rose."

The article called the water supply of the lost river inexhaustible and spoke of the great climate in which four or five crops a year could be raised instead of the one or two that could be raised by farmers in the East and North. The article concludes, "This is why these farmers are ever eager to migrate to the Southwest where there are no long dreary winters that prevent them from working and adding to their savings."

The article was right about some things, wrong about others. The Mimbres could have been called a lost river at that time; it is a lovely mountain stream that rises in the Black Range, winds its way through the foothills, and flows into the flat country of Luna County, which is on the northern edge of Mexico's high

Chihuahuan Desert. In years of heavy rain and snowfall, the Mimbres can turn this flat land into a vast floodplain. But in normal or dry years the volume of the Mimbres' water becomes less and less and soon sinks into the arid ground until there is no discernible riverbed. The water continues to flow as a subterranean river, however; in that sense it is "lost," as it mingles with other underground runoff water from nearby mountain ranges.

The Mimbres was also lost in the sense that for a long time no one realized that the vast underground drainage could be tapped for irrigation. The *El Paso Morning Times* article was wrong that the settlers had irrigated farms in the 1880s. Wells for drinking water and watering vegetable gardens were dug then, but it was not until about 1909 that the idea of pumping the underground water for large-scale irrigation was put into practice.

Frank Smyer's grandfather homesteaded east of Deming in the early 1890s. In an informal family history, one of Frank's aunts, Virgia Smyer Nunn, wrote about the days when she was a girl on the homestead. "The Mimbres River ran every winter and spring and flooded all our land. Father would cut and bale tons of native hay each year. It was hauled to Deming or Carne, New Mexico, and shipped to Hyde Brothers, and the Army in El Paso. He always had real good work horses, which he was very proud of.

"In 1910, the first big irrigation well was drilled on our land, and in 1912, a 35-horsepower diesel engine was installed. To see that beautiful stream of water was really something. We put in fields of alfalfa, milo maize, and raised hogs for a few years. And more native hay each year."

The Smyers combined ranching with farming and, according to Virgia Smyer Nunn, thought of their valley as a "land of sunshine and honey." The combining of ranching and farming was probably a wise move economically because, according to Robert F. Miller in *The History of Luna County*, many early farmers did not have the same success that the Smyer family had.

"The Mimbres valley region was a rich land for exploitation," Miller says. "Land companies were organized and expensive machinery was sold to farmers unacquainted with western agricultural methods. This state of activity and apparent prosperity continued until about 1914 or 1915, when farmers realized they could not produce their crops at a profit. Many farms were abandoned within the next few years."

Aylmer Ruebush grew up in Deming and has been farming on the edge of town for fifty years. "In '18 there were twelve thousand people in this valley," he told us. "Homesteads with little school-houses scattered all over at Sunshine, Capitol Dome, Waterloo, Luxor, Hermanas. Nothing left of them now but foundations. The homesteaders got 160 acres. They came in and built homes, put in their life savings. They couldn't make a living on 160 acres. And there was no place to sell their produce.

"By the early '30s lots of them had to sell out or they just pulled out. Their little old houses gradually fell apart. Tax title hunters came in and bought up land that had been forfeited for nonpayment of taxes. A man with some cash could buy land that way for almost nothing and just hold it."

Agricultural statistics tell the same story and add another dimension. In 1910 there were 340 farms in Luna County, only eight of them with more than one thousand acres. By 1920 the number of farms in the county had dropped to 287 but 44 of them were larger than 1,000 acres. Today there are less than 200 farms in the county, but most are from several hundred acres to over a thousand. This pattern of fewer farms of larger acreage has become common in all parts of the United States.

Besides larger farms, another important change came to Luna County agriculture. "This country was brought back by turbine pumps," Aylmer Ruebush said to us. "They made it easier to draw water from deeper wells."

Everyone agrees with Aylmer about that. The old centrifugal pump was less efficient, more expensive to operate, and needed repair more often than the turbine pump that came into general use in the 1940s. Modern technology was critical in making large-scale irrigation by well water a paying business, but other things helped.

Trucks and better highways opened up new markets. World War II and the postwar boom brought increased demands for food both in the United States and worldwide.

Farmers went into a period of relative prosperity during the sixties and early seventies, not only in southwest New Mexico but over most of the country. A wave of excitement and rising expectations washed over the agricultural world.

From their farm east of Deming, Fannie and Frank Smyer watched it all happen. "There was so much farm hype in the early seventies," Fannie told us. "The experts said America was going to feed the world. The government urged farmers to expand as much and as fast as they could. Banks made it easy for farmers to borrow money. People who should have known better were saying to farmers, 'Get big or get out.' And farmers started saying it to each other."

Some instinct, Fannie said, told Frank not to go along with all the hype. Resisting was hard when he saw so many of his friends and fellow farmers plunging, borrowing money to buy more land and newer equipment. But Frank decided that he had all the land he could work properly, and he managed to keep his old equipment working. He borrowed from the bank no more than he needed to keep going.

"More than once," Fannie remembers, "he said to me, 'Maybe it's not get big *or* get out. Maybe it's going to be, 'Get big *and* get out.'"

And time proved Frank tragically right. By the mid-1970s the bubble had burst: the Arab oil embargo sent energy costs—gasoline, diesel fuel, electricity—skyrocketing; fertilizers jumped dramatically in price; sharply rising interest rates made bank loans a perilous risk. At the same time the inflated dollar made American products—including farm products—hard to sell overseas. A U.S. government embargo on selling grain to Russia further complicated the financial picture for many farmers.

The result was that banks began to foreclose on farms for non-payment of loans. Some farmers declared bankruptcy. Some farms simply went out of production. Luna County was part of a farm crisis that engulfed the entire nation.

"It was scary," Fannie Smyer said. "It still is." And then she used a simile I have not forgotten. "Farmers were like stars being sucked into an economic black hole."

I talked with Earl Spruiell, president of the First New Mexico Bank in Deming. He acknowledged the hard times, not only for farmers but also for ranchers. "There never was a ranch around here in Chapter Eleven until four years ago," he said, referring to the federal bankruptcy law.

He spoke of the early seventies. "We were caught up in some good years then. This has always been a conservative country, but some farmers got deep in debt. Then costs and interest rates went up. A tractor that cost $16,000 then costs $60,000 now. The farmers and ranchers who went under were the ones who couldn't service their debt. The survivors are the ones who don't owe a lot of money—the conservative ones."

As the bank president talked, I thought about Frank Smyer and the others like him who had decided that they didn't have to get out if they didn't get big. It is true that the trend of American agriculture is toward bigger farms, but clearly how big and how fast are questions that every farmer, depending on his own circumstances, must find the right answers to.

Later we went to see Emmanual Vocale who lives in a graceful Spanish-style house on the old road to Lordsburg. We met him just as he was walking in from a pond with a shotgun over one shoulder. He shoots an occasional duck or goose for the table (this was in November). Vocale's father, an Italian immigrant, came to Luna County in the twenties with his family and began farming immediately.

Emmanual Vocale bought forty acres in 1934 and was married three years later. He raised milo, cotton, beans, and vegetables. "I learned vegetable growing from a Japanese truck farmer," he said. "Vegetables are a funny crop. One year you get rich, the next you make nothing."

Over time Vocale expanded to one thousand acres by buying up farms around him. In the early 1940s he began growing grapes,

Emmanual Vocale

partly because his father had planted vines soon after coming to New Mexico. Vocale quit farming ten years ago and just tends his grapes now.

Despite the present difficult economic conditions, he is optimistic about Luna County's and Deming's future. "Things will never get as bad as they were during the Depression," he said. "Agriculture will come back."

Mr. Vocale smiled. "Why, even now if you have your farm paid for and your equipment paid for, you can make as much as you can working for wages."

Born to the Land

ONE day Frank showed us around the Smyer farm, which is located in a part of Luna County known as Lewis Flats. The area was named for C. S. Lewis, Frank's maternal great grandfather, who homesteaded near Deming in the late 1880s. Frank's paternal grandfather, John R. Smyer, homesteaded at the same time, and the two families, related by marriage, were the first in this section of the Mimbres Valley. Frank and Fannie's farm of four hundred acres contains the original Smyer homestead. Frank has lived on this land all his life.

"Ever since I was a little boy, I knew I wanted to be a farmer," Frank told us. "I love to watch a seed turn into a plant. I don't know words to describe how I feel. Out here early in the morning, before the sun comes up, and I'm changing the water from one field to another, there is a wonderful smell to the soil. Farming is so many things besides money to me. It's just something I have to do."

We stopped to look at a stand of young wheat. To our inexperienced eyes it looked fine, but Frank showed us where bugs were

Frank examining young wheat for disease

eating it and where some frosty mornings had caused the ends of the plants to turn brown. He called this "tip burn."

Frank's main cash crop is chile. "I just raise enough wheat to stay in the government program," he said, "and enough cotton to keep up the family tradition. I raise milo, too. I try to diversify so I'll get at least one good crop."

Tradition is important to Frank, just as it is to Joe Bill Nunn. "We have a hundred years of family history wrapped up in this land," Frank said.

He showed us some of his equipment. "That tractor cost $18,000 when I bought it in '77," he said, pointing to his International Harvester. "Now it's about $50,000. You can't keep up with that. I buy all my equipment secondhand. There's lots of equipment being auctioned off these days by fellows going out of business."

Frank still has a tractor that his father bought in 1947. "You have

Strings of dried chile called ristras *hang on the porches of thousands of New Mexican homes. New Mexicans eat more chile per capita than any other Americans. Chile is one of New Mexico's official state symbols; the other is the pinto bean. The spelling* chile *is preferred to* chili *in New Mexico.*

to make your equipment last because you don't have the capital to keep renewing it," he said.

Frank admits that he keeps his father's tractor partly for sentimental reasons, but he has no such feelings about the 1971 pickup he drives. He keeps it running because it saves him the price of a new one. "I don't need the smell of new paint," he says. "I have to know how to weld, be a mechanic, an electrician, a vet—lots of different trades." On the subject of equipment again Frank said, "Years ago all the neighbors around here would throw in and help each other. One would have a thrasher, another a bean cutter. But after the war farmers became independent and went their separate ways. Now we're reverting to our old ways because we can't afford all the equipment we need. It's kind of nice."

We talked about water. That old article in the *El Paso Morning Times* was wrong about something else: the water in the Mimbres Valley drainage was not "inexhaustible." The more the prairie was ploughed and crops planted, Frank said, the more the water table dropped and the deeper the wells had to be dug. To bring about control, water-rights laws were passed. Water was rationed according to cultivated acreage, and after a certain time no more water rights were issued.

Now some acreage carries water rights, but most land does not. Land with water rights is expensive; land on which irrigation is not allowed is relatively cheap, but except in special cases it cannot be used for farming. Strict limits are put on the amount of water a farmer is allowed to use. Water-use records must be maintained, and airplanes check on land being irrigated.

"So the water table is slowly rising," Frank said, "but that depends on rainfall, too."

Sometimes it is hard to ask a question that may seem foolish, but I learned long ago that—if I can't figure out the answer—it is better to ask it. I did that now.

"I understand about the water table," I said, "but except for that, why do farmers here need rain since you water your crops through irrigation?"

"Plants need to take in moisture through humidity as well as from irrigation," Frank said. "There has to be some rain if you're going to have a good crop. Another thing: with good rain you can grow some crops on nonirrigated land. Just 310 of my acres have water rights, so growing crops anywhere else depends on rain and flood water from the Mimbres."

We asked Frank if he had considered growing lettuce and onions, as some farmers were doing. Again Frank showed the cautious nature that is keeping him in the farming business. Lettuce and onions are very high risk ventures, he told us. Last year half the lettuce crop was discarded at the local packing shed because of a glut on the market.

"You might do all right," Frank said, "but then again you could take your money to Las Vegas and not lose it any faster."

ONE morning Paul and I went early to the Smyers' house. Paul wanted to get some pictures of Frank on his tractor, and the two of them went off to the fields together. I stayed in the warm kitchen, drank coffee, and talked to Fannie. It was natural that our conversation should turn first to Frank.

"He was born to the land," Fannie said. "His determination has kept us here even though there were times it might have made more sense to run."

Fannie recalled the terror of impending bankruptcy seven years ago. The profit was gone from cotton and grain. The cost of electricity, fertilizer, insecticides was rising wildly, and bank interest rates were at an all-time high. They had to have a moneymaking crop if they were going to survive.

"My husband doesn't change easily, but his back was against the wall," Fannie said. "He decided to try a chile crop. That was the turning point. Chile has made all the difference for us."

About the time I was starting on my third cup of coffee, Kelly Smyer and her sister Katherine, both in the throes of getting ready for school, came into the kitchen. They poured orange juice and

The Smyer family: Frank, Katherine, Fannie, Karla, Kelly

milk for themselves and ate big bowls of cold cereal. At that time Kelly was sixteen and a junior at Deming High School; Katherine was eight, a third-grader. Frank and Fannie have a third daughter, Karla, who was twenty and working in California at the time of Paul's and my visit.

"I'm exploding the myth of the big farm breakfast," Fannie said. "No sausage and eggs, potatoes and grits and biscuits and gravy in this house. Everyone is on their own for breakfast."

Katherine catches the school bus, which stops right in front of the house, to her elementary school in Deming. Kelly, however, has an old hand-me-down car that she drives to Deming High School. This means that she can make a more leisurely departure for school in the mornings and stay for school activities or visit with town friends after school.

Giving the old family car or pickup to the high-school-age son or daughter seems to be what many ranch and farm families do if they can afford to. It gives their teenagers mobility that makes up, at least in part, for not living in town close to friends.

"Farm kids live like all the other kids now," Fannie said.

Kelly recently had a major part in the high school production of *Brigadoon*. Fannie said that she and Frank were almost too nervous to go. But Kelly turned in a stellar performance, and all their friends came around to congratulate them.

Fannie is full of energy and has a good sense of humor. A few years ago she decided to run for the office of county treasurer; since it is an elective office, she had to conduct a political campaign with hand-shaking, speeches, and question-and-answer sessions with voters. Fannie has a background in accounting, but when anyone wanted to know her qualifications for being county treasurer, she said that her best answer was, "I helped an American farmer survive the farm crisis."

She won the election.

In fact, the Smyer family has been in Luna County politics for three generations. Frank's father and brother served as county commissioner, his uncle and cousin as sheriff. "I really appreciated having a good job while times were so hard," Fannie said, "and I appreciated the people of this county entrusting me with an office that important.

"But every afternoon I would drive home, and as I came over the hill and into this valley, I would feel sad about what I was missing out on."

Fannie looked out the window. "I love being here with Frank and the kids. If I ever have to go back to work in town, I will, of course. But I hope I never have to."

A small state highway runs beside the Smyer farm. On the other side of the highway is a beautiful estate with rows of trees that I took to be some kind of orchard. There is a fine brick house on the land, and a road lined with poplar trees leads to the house. When I asked Fannie about this place, she said that it belongs to an Iranian prince, one of the royal family that was forced to flee from Iran when the Shah was toppled.

"He lives in California but visits here sometimes," Fannie said. "I understand the country around here reminds him of Iran. And those trees. They're pistachio trees. I think they remind him of Iran, too."

The prince bought forty acres of unimproved mesquite land from Frank and Fannie for what Fannie considered an absurdly high price. "But I recovered long enough to bank the check," she said. "It sure took a chunk out of our indebtedness."

The prince clearly spared no cost in developing his new estate just the way he wanted it. Fannie said he even bought some water rights on land elsewhere and had them transferred to the land on his estate.

I thought that kind of movement of water rights was against the law and said so to Fannie. Apparently Frank and Fannie thought so, too, and were concerned that the additional water use in this area might adversely affect the water table. They took the matter to court.

"Imagine," Fannie said. "The paupers sued the prince."

But the court ruled in favor of the prince, and he moved his water rights.

By the time Frank and Paul returned from the field, a strong wind was beginning to batter the house. Paul had had trouble taking pictures because of the dust. "It used to be like this a lot," Fannie said. "I can remember in '67 watching Frank ride away from the house and disappearing instantly. Ten feet away he was invisible. The first years of our marriage I felt like we were living in the Sahara."

Frank said, "I've been in dust so bad that I couldn't even see the front of my pickup."

"But the cycle was broken in '72 when the Mimbres flooded the valley for the first time in many years," Fannie said. "We had water two hundred feet from our back door. Since then the river has flooded five more times."

Breaking her rule, Fannie offered to cook breakfast, and no one protested. While she was frying bacon and eggs, making toast, setting out preserves, and doing another pot of coffee, she said, "In 1962 in high school I was named Betty Crocker Homemaker of Tomorrow. How's that for a joke?"

As I ate the good breakfast, I didn't think it was a joke at all. When we came to dinner a few nights later, Fannie served a magnificent roast beef with roasted red chiles from the Smyer farm. Then I was sure that the Betty Crocker Award had been well placed.

LIKE his grandfather in the 1890s, Frank runs a small cattle operation as part of his farming business. He has a "pasture" of four sections adjacent to the farm, 2,560 acres, on which he keeps a herd of sixty "mother cows." He runs the cows in this pasture, which has good tobosa grass and yucca plant forage, from March until November. Then, when harvest is over, the cows graze on the stalks and other residue of the chile, cotton, wheat, and milo acreage. The calf crop, which averages about fifty a year, provides a reliable extra income for the Smyer farm.

The Smyers do not raise pigs commercially, but the Smyer name has become associated with some high quality porkers in Luna County. As part of their Future Farmers of America (FFA) activities, both Kelly and Karla, when she was in high school, raised pigs and had many prize-winning entries in the Southwestern New Mexico State Fair livestock shows.

But the aftermath of the shows has not always been easy. The practice is that all animals entered are sold to the packer for slaughter after the judging. The winner commands the highest prices naturally, but all livestock are sold, regardless of whether they place in the competition. The problem is that, from months of feeding and caring for their pigs from the time they were small and cute, Karla and Kelly have sometimes become quite attached to them. Seeing them trucked off to become pork chops is often a very low moment in the whole process.

One pig—Fannie described him as a "gentle, friendly old hog"—particularly won Kelly's heart. He did not win a ribbon in the show,

Kelly Smyer with her friendly pig

but when the time came for him to be shipped away, Kelly was quite depressed. She was standing at the pen talking with some of the other FFA members, her arm dangling over the pen rail, when the pig tugged gently at her FFA jacket sleeve.

That was too much. Kelly went to the FFA adviser and told him that she didn't want to sell her pig. That couldn't be, she was told; the rule was that all animals go to the packer. At that point Fannie interceded for Kelly and was able to save the pig. Today he is an aging, content—still gentle and friendly—resident of the farm, living comfortably in a pen just west of the Smyer house.

In her senior year Kelly is too busy to enter the livestock show; among other distractions, she has the lead role, the part played by Marilyn Monroe, in the Deming High School production of *Bus Stop*. But Katherine is now old enough to enter the state fair competition, and her father will soon help her pick out her first pig to raise.

"We've Always Been a Close Family"

I F we hadn't gone into pecans in '56, we probably wouldn't have survived," Alton Milligan said. "We made good money on our cotton for awhile, but then synthetics took care of that market. When my dad bought this place there were only two trees on it. And talk about poor. We were poor folks! We had an outside privy, and we had to pack our water."

We were sitting in the kitchen of Alton Milligan's nice house early on a Sunday morning, drinking coffee and listening to him talk about growing pecans. Down the road just a bit is the house of his father and mother, Robert and Margaret Milligan. Their house is surrounded by some lovely cottonwoods and a 160-acre grove of fine pecan trees. Down another dusty farm road, only a quarter of a mile away, lives Alton's sister, Diana Milligan, on a 140-acre farm that she bought only recently. She is growing chiles and lettuce on the farm, which hadn't been worked in over ten years.

The Milligan pecan grove, located on the southern edge of Deming, produces half a million pounds of nuts yearly. Most of the nuts are sold to the Planters Peanuts Company in San Antonio, Texas, but some are shipped to plants in Georgia. One reason that this part of Luna County is good pecan country, we learned, is that it does not have the insect problem that many southern states have; drier climate and colder winters take care of bugs that attack pecan trees in other places. New Mexico has become the third largest pecan-growing state, behind Georgia and Texas. Recent drought in Georgia has driven up prices to where pecan kernels now sell for $1.00 a pound.

Despite the good price paid for pecans, there are only three or four other growers in the Deming area because of the time and money required to get into pecan farming. Alton's father bought the land for the pecan groves in 1946; but it took ten years to save and borrow enough money to level the land, test soil, drill wells, and

(Above) Three generations of the Milligan family: Diana, Margaret, Robert, Alton, Kelly

(Left) Pedro Mirmontez, a worker on the Milligan pecan farm

finally to plant an initial three thousand trees. After that it took eight years of watering to get the pecan trees to the point of producing. That is a long time to wait for a return on your money and labor.

Harvesting pecans—a two-month job in the Milligan grove—is also expensive, requiring three big, expensive machines. We watched all three in action that morning. A shaker fastens a long arm on the tree trunk and then vibrates with so much energy that the ground quivers for several yards around. A great shower of leaves and nuts comes down while the shaking is going on. A sweeper then makes long windrows of leaves and nuts, and a harvester sucks them up, discarding the leaves.

About the only unskilled manual labor in harvesting pecans today is from workers who do final inspection as nuts travel down a conveyer belt. But Alton's sister Diana recalls a time when human labor did all the things that machines do now. "I remember when we planted our first pecan trees years ago," she told us. "We dug holes for days. When the trees started to bear, we climbed up in them and knocked the nuts down with yucca sticks. Then we picked them up and put them in bags."

The Milligan pecan farm remains very much a family operation. At seventy-two, Robert Milligan still puts in a full day on farm business. "If there isn't something for him to do, he invents it," says Alton, speaking of his father. "I wish I could get him to slow down a bit, but there's no way."

The elder Milligan is quietly proud of what he and his family have accomplished. "We've always been a close family," he told us with some satisfaction the first time we visited him at his house. "We meet here every morning, grab a cup of coffee, and decide what we're going to do."

The "we" includes Alton and Alton's two strapping sons, Kelly and Terry, who are in their early twenties and want to be farmers, too. Kelly graduated from high school in 1984 and says he knew from an early age that farming was his destiny. He has tried working in Montana, California, and New York, but always the pull of family, farm, and the southwestern country he grew up in brings him back.

(Above) Robert Milligan and Wolf

(Right) Harvesting pecans is a highly mechanized operation. Here a shaker creates a shower of leaves and nuts.

"If I leave for a week or two, I'm already homesick," he says. "I can't wait to get back."

Kelly has been living in Deming, but he wants to buy a trailer and move back to the farm. "I'm tired of town," he told us. "It's too noisy."

Diana managed a Kampgrounds of America (KOA) in Deming for several years and lived in Las Vegas for five years, where she ran a small casino. "I couldn't wait to get back," she said, echoing Kelly's words. "There you were just a number, didn't even know your neighbors. Here you walk down the street and talk to everybody."

And Diana added, "The nice thing about farm families is that they find things for their kids to do and keep them close."

The Milligan family is marked not only by a physical closeness but also by an emotional closeness that shows in the pride that Diana takes in her father. "My father is a self-made man," she told us. "He has only an eighth-grade education. He grew up on a ranch out in the middle of nowhere. When I was young he was very strict with me; I couldn't go out the door until he checked my appearance. We always worked together as a family and achieved as a family. My children are growing up the same way. When I had the KOA the kids would come home right after school and start working."

About her new farm, Diana says, "If there is a piece of equipment I can't run, there's somebody in the family who will help. My dad comes by at least twice a day to see that I'm doing things right."

We visited Diana on her farm one Saturday morning as she was hoeing tiny plants of her first lettuce crop; her daughter Shannon and son-in-law Carl, who is a deputy sheriff, were helping her. "You have to be happy on a morning like this," Diana said. "It's so beautiful. A little earlier we could hear the quail calling out back. Buying this place took a lot of faith, but I knew my brother and father were beside me."

Another morning Margaret Milligan talked to us about their early days in farming. In the beginning and while they were waiting for the pecan trees to produce, they raised cotton, beans, alfalfa, and other crops. They still grow beans and cotton but only as a side line.

Diana Milligan on her farm. Her daughter and son-in-law help.

"Our first house was two rooms," she said. "We built it mainly with wooden practice-bomb crates discarded by the Air Force base that was here during World War II. We just hauled them over here and used them like adobe bricks. They were about that size—four feet by eight inches.

"We cooked with butane and lit the house with kerosene lamps. Alton and Diana carried water from the well for us to use here in the house. We had one old milk cow, and we leased a Ford tractor when we needed it."

Mrs. Milligan summed up their early hand-to-mouth existence in this way, "It was a good life, but I wouldn't want to do it again."

DURING our April visit Robert Milligan took us for a drive through the pecan grove in his battered old pickup; his hound, Wolf, hopped in back and came along uninvited. Mr. Milligan gave us a running commentary as we followed dirt roads through the trees, stopping occasionally while he checked a pump, an irrigation ditch, the soil.

On irrigation methods: "We seep water through the trees real slow. I like to hold the water on them for twenty hours once a month until summer comes along and then we drop down to every fifteen days."

About pruning trees: "We start pruning when they reach twenty-five years. Takes four years for a tree to come back and then they'll be like a brand new tree. Pecan trees have a long life and will produce as long as you take care of them."

On fertilizer and energy costs: "We have 9,800 trees now. We use seventy thousand pounds of fertilizer every year. That's expensive. But our biggest expense is electricity. Energy costs go up and up."

Mr. Milligan's conversation is full of facts about soil analysis, leaf research, water tables, fertilizers, pump capacity. But there is another side to him, the side of a man who simply loves to be outdoors and with nature. As we drove he pointed out large piles of tree trimmings and said, "That's where my quail live."

I asked Mr. Milligan how he first got the idea of going into pecan farming.

"Dean Stahmann," he said.

I had seen the vast Stahmann pecan groves around Las Cruces and knew that they had been in production for well over half a century. "He got you started?" I asked.

"I wasn't farming then," Mr. Milligan said. "That was over forty years ago. I was working for the New Mexico Highway Department and doing some other things. One day I delivered a load of lumber to the Stahmann headquarters. I met Dean Stahmann, the owner, by accident. Turned out he knew my dad. He asked me to stay for lunch, and we talked about growing pecans. When I left, he said, 'Bob, I think you would make a good green-thumb farmer.'"

Robert Milligan studied one of his severely pruned pecan trees. "Maybe I did," he said.

Aylmer

WE first went to see Aylmer Ruebush because we had heard that he runs a motel for cattle. It didn't turn out to be that, but almost: Aylmer calls his business the Deming Cattle Rest. It is located on his farm east of town and has been in operation for thirty-five years. Federal interstate law requires that cattle being shipped by truck must have a break in their journey at least once every twenty-four hours so they can be fed, watered, and have a chance to move around.

"We're right on the highway to California, so it makes a good place for truckers to stop," Aylmer said.

I understood the humane law about giving cattle a chance to eat, drink, and rest, but I didn't understand why they would be coming from the east into cattle country.

"Cattle from Mississippi, Alabama, Arkansas, Tennessee, and other places stop here," Aylmer said. "Yearlings have to put on weight in feedlots, and the biggest feedlots in the country are in the Imperial Valley in California."

I should have known that since Paul and I had spent some time in the Imperial Valley the year before. We had seen the vast agricultural output of what is surely one of the world's greatest natural hothouses, irrigated with water from the Boulder and Imperial dams. Alfalfa is grown there for the cattle, Aylmer explained, and they eat the "garbage" from the vegetable farms: scrap lettuce leaves, carrot tops, and other leftovers.

The cattle-rest corrals are right beside the Ruebush house, and they have provided a good income for Aylmer and his wife, June, over the years; but, first and last, the Ruebushes are a farm couple. Aylmer tells a familiar story of starting out poor.

"My wife, June—the June bug—and me started out with nothing—no water, no bathroom. We put in every post, every board, and just built it up over the years. We farmed here for almost fifty years."

*June and Aylmer Ruebush. They met in church and were married in 1939. "We were poor,"
Aylmer says. "Our entertainment was going around to different churches and singing."
Church work remains important in their lives.*

Aylmer speaks with affection about "this little old piece of land," which is irrigated by just two wells. "I'm lucky," he said. "My water is shallow here—just 140 feet—because I'm backed up against the river. That's where the good land is, where the river had laid down silt for millions of years."

Aylmer is retired from farming now and rents the fields around his house to his son Stafford, who is the only one of the five Ruebush children working as a farmer. Stafford Ruebush, following the current trend, has concentrated on raising chiles. In October and November fields of mature red chiles surround the Ruebush house, glistening in the bright fall sunlight.

We talked to Aylmer about the early days. He was born on the "home place" just east of Deming in 1916, the ninth of eleven brothers. He has a photograph taken in the mid-1960s showing the brothers lined up like a football team.

"My father was a farmer in Texas," Aylmer said. "He heard about Deming and came here to investigate. He got off the train in '06 and just stayed."

Aylmer's father first ran a livery stable and then became a grocer, starting a store called Ruebush Market. All of the sons took their turns working behind the counter; Aylmer learned butchering there. He remembers the lean times that began in the late twenties and got worse in the thirties.

"Nobody had any money in those days," he said. "Everybody bought on credit, and my father couldn't turn anybody down. We went broke. We had to pay cash for our groceries because we couldn't get any credit. The only people who had any cash were the Mexican railroad crews that worked east and west of town. They'd come into town late on Saturday night after they got their pay. We'd stay open until they came in about nine o'clock. We had to have some cash."

According to Aylmer, he became a farmer at the age of twelve. "Mrs. Avant came to our store one day," he said. "She had 320 acres east of town, and she asked my father if he would trade her $5,000 worth of credit at the store for that land. He said yes, and one of my

Dust storms like this one occur in Luna County in late winter and spring, but they are not as frequent or as severe as they were earlier in this century.

brothers and me started farming there. I've been a farmer ever since."

Aylmer has vivid memories of the Dust Bowl years of the early 1930s. "Big clouds of red dust would be coming out of Oklahoma," he said, "and by noon it would be settling in here like everything. Terrible winds would blow out there in those old fields. Dirt would pile up along the fencerows. Horses could hardly move against that wind. Dust balls would come out of their eyes and roll right down their cheeks. One Sunday five windmills blew over. You had to be pretty tough to stay in this country. You still do."

Inevitably Aylmer's thoughts turned to drought and rain. "In the early thirties it just quit raining. One year I didn't get two and a half inches. It's been so dry here that even mesquite bushes died. Ol' broomweed has taken over. Maybe it's startin' to turn around. We had sixteen-seventeen inches last year."

Aylmer thought a moment before adding, "I've always said it rains everywhere else, and if the good Lord has any left, He sends it here."

I couldn't help asking, "Do you wish you had grown up somewhere else?"

Aylmer looked at me. "This is home," he said.

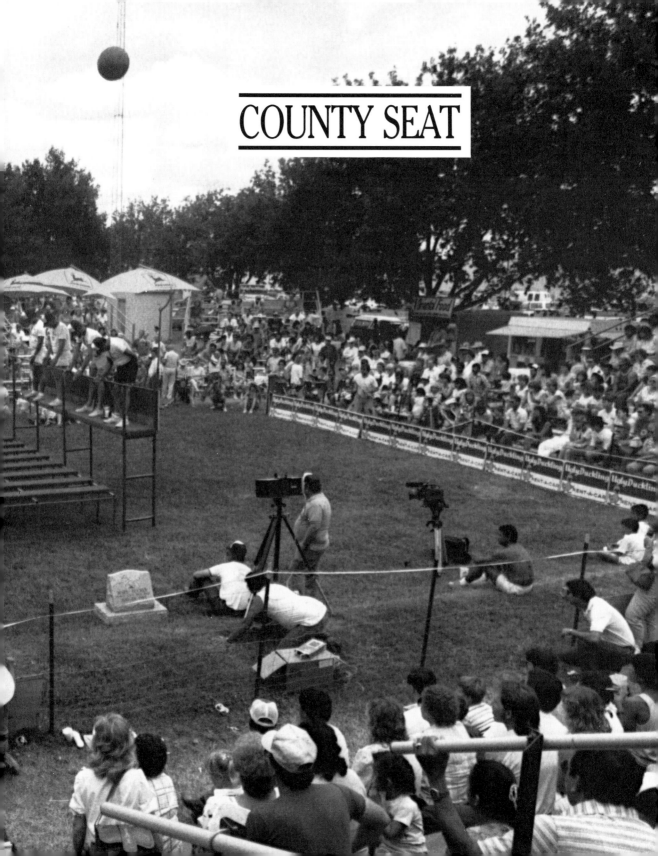

COUNTY SEAT

Painting faces at the Deming spring festival

THE day we arrived in Deming to begin our April visit the merchants' association was having a spring festival, so we joined in the fun. The Merry Mixers square dance club was putting on a demonstration in one of the blocked-off streets. In a big parking lot, students from Dance Studio 87 were doing the same, dressed in bright costumes for the occasion. They were followed by the white-uniformed karate students showing what they had learned about martial arts from the local Kung Fu master.

Families from town, ranch, and farm were there, greeting each other, standing around talking, looking in shop windows. The young kids were having the best time, which is the way it should be. Gas-filled balloons were handed out, and a young woman outside a store called the Doll Shop was painting masks with theatrical paint on every youngster who came around.

Women from civic clubs and churches were holding bake sales, their sidewalk tables loaded with cakes and cookies. I ate my way up one side of the street and down the other just to be friendly. When I found Paul at the hot dog and hamburger stand, run I think by the Lions Club or the American Legion, I wasn't hungry.

In truth, the spring festival wasn't a big deal; but everyone seemed to have a good time, and the merchants had a chance to show off their spring wares and maybe make a few extra sales.

Even if I hadn't known that this ranching and farming country was going through economic tough times, I could have guessed it from walking around Deming. It wasn't becoming a ghost town, nothing like that certainly, but there were more empty stores, more building-for-rent signs, than you would expect to see in an economically healthy climate. From talking to Frank and Fannie Smyer later, I learned that thirty-six stores have gone out of business in the past few years and that three farm implement businesses have shrunk to one.

When we talked to Shanty Bowman, a Deming insurance agent who has seen lots of the town's economic ups and downs, he spoke of cotton prices that have been depressed for the last six or eight years and about high electricity costs that hurt farmers who irrigate with electric pumps. He also said that the young grape industry in Luna County is undercapitalized and faces strong competition from other parts of the country.

"I'm down on Deming at the moment," Bowman said. "I don't know if it will ever come back."

Earl Spruiell, the First New Mexico Bank president, acknowledged the hard times but said, "Deming is not fixing to fold up. It's a tougher economy than that."

At Deming High School, Bayne Anderson put things in perspective for us, just as a good history teacher should. "Deming has always been a town looking for its star," he said.

In the beginning, Anderson explained, the star was the Southern Pacific; people thought it would make Deming a great railroad center. The railroad was important, but mainly because it brought ranchers in. Then Deming citizens thought mining would make their town into a big city, but that didn't happen. Next, farming created great expectations in the Mimbres Valley but, like ranching, had its good times and bad.

World War I brought a big Army installation, Camp Cody, to Deming, and World War II brought an Air Force base; these two

Ballet class at Dance Studio 87. As the name suggests, the dance school is a new addition to Deming.

military establishments were responsible for waves of prosperity in Deming, but after the wars, they were soon gone.

During the 1960s manufacturing came to Deming; the town's largest employer during that period was the Auburn Rubber Company, a maker of plastic toys. But after a few years, the company moved to another location. Deming built an industrial park, but few industries were attracted to it after the Auburn Rubber Company left.

Railroads, mining, military bases, industry all had their place in Deming's development; but over the decades, across a hundred years, ranching and farming, with all their ups and downs, provided the bedrock that the town could build on.

Larry and Joemarie Semprevivo came to Deming from New Jersey ten years ago because of Larry's arthritis. Larry has invented a sugar-free ice cream which he is having some success in marketing. Making more than a bare living in Deming is hard, Larry says, but he adds, "It's a real friendly town where we know everybody. I truly believe that everybody looks after my son as though he were their own."

With a population of ten thousand, Deming today is a good-sized town; two-thirds of Luna County's residents live there, and Deming has always been the economic and social hub of the county. It has seven elementary schools which feed into the junior high and high school and over forty churches of many denominations. It has some things you might not expect in a town of its size: a good historical museum staffed mainly by volunteers and a very active arts council that brings in music and drama programs and puts on arts and crafts exhibits.

Deming is not big enough to have suffered an invasion of fast-food franchises, but Dairy Queen, Kentucky Fried Chicken, and McDonald's have established beachheads. Its location two hours west of El Paso and three hours east of Tucson has made Deming a good stopping place for travelers on Interstate 10. By my informal count fifteen motels located in town and on the outskirts buoy the local economy.

But one does not stay in Deming long without realizing that it is essentially a Western ranching and farming town. The crisp desert air, the feel of the flat prairie, the sight of nearby mountains are a part of Deming. Pickup trucks are much in evidence on the streets as ranchers and farmers come in to do their business. Deming has three boot shops, at least one saddle shop, and—in good times—several farm equipment stores.

A weekly cattle sale and auction brings buyers from beyond Luna County. The Southwestern New Mexico State Fair which takes place each October in Deming features cattle shows. For the past fifteen years a Butterfield Trail Days festival has been held in the courtyard park, and a big roping contest is held on Labor Day week-end. Every issue of the *Deming Headlight,* the local daily newspaper, devotes a generous amount of space to ranching and farming news and feature stories.

Another thing that comes through to you soon is that the people of Deming and the ranchers and farmers of Luna County are comfortable with their town. They like it and they trust it. Las Cruces, a vigorous city of fifty-five thousand, is less than an hour from

111

Jack Neeley, a Deming saddlemaker

Deming; El Paso, a major city of half a million, is less than two hours away. These two urban magnets might be expected to drain much of the economic and social life from Deming, but that has not happened.

Shoppers are sometimes lured to the cities, but Deming still is home to the people who live there and to most other Luna County residents. They know everyone and everyone knows them. Deming is their place.

"People Care About You Here"

THE day I met with the ranch women at the museum, Paul talked with a group of students at Deming High School. They all had definite views about their town; Paul Grimm, who was born in South Korea and lived first in Tucson, and then in Deming, expressed a feeling that most of them held.

"You get the idea that everybody cares about you in Deming," he said. "And the school is a microcosm of the town. When my parents told me we were moving to Deming, I thought, Oh, it's going to be awful. But now I'm glad we came."

"I was the same way," said Joseph Semprevivo, whose family came from New Jersey ten years ago because of the father's health. "I thought, Man, will Deming ever be boring. But it's just what you make it. It doesn't have to be dull. Like the desert. We go there on weekends. There's lots to do outdoors."

Herb Borden is a farm boy who sees no future for himself in farming. He would like to go into law enforcement or environmental work and thinks he will have to leave Deming to get the training and find what he is looking for. "But I'd like for my kids to live here and go to school here if I could come back to a good steady job," he said.

The talk turned to the future, and Paul asked the students if they thought they would still be in Deming in ten years' time.

"We won't be here then," Paul Grimm said. "Deming is a nice place to grow up in, but the best thing to do is to go off to college and find a job somewhere else."

Everyone agreed. They all said that they wanted to see the outside world and what lies beyond the Interstate. There was a general feeling that Deming could not supply what they were looking for. NGai Williams, who is a part of Deming's very small black community, plans to join the navy after high school and would like to be a nuclear physicist someday. Senior class treasurer Lorraine Parra, a Hispanic, wants to be a hair designer. Hernando Sanchez, also Hispanic, hopes to qualify for West Point. Vicki Wilcox, president of the junior class, wants to study political science and end up in Washington as New Mexico's first woman senator. She classifies herself as a conservative liberal.

Some of the group did not rule out the possibility of returning to Deming, but no one seemed to have confidence that it could provide reasonable job opportunities for young people in the future. "Deming has tremendous economic potential," NGai Williams said, "located as it is on the Interstate and close enough to the border so it could be an entry point for goods coming north."

"Deming needs industry to improve," Joseph Semprevivo added.

But Herb Borden, even though he sees no future in farming for himself, has a clear view of the place where he was born and raised. "You can't change our way of life that easily," he said. "Deming is here mainly for the sake of agriculture, and that's just the way it is. You wouldn't expect New York City to become an agricultural center."

While the group's overall feeling for Deming was one of affection, they were not oblivious to some small-town problems. One was the need to find ways to keep active. That, the students said, was the secret of contentment in a town of Deming's size. Their solution was to be involved in school activities; all were members of one or more

114

Deming High School students: Back row from left, Vicki Wilcox, Lorraine Perra, Herb Borden, Paul Grimm. Front row from left, Joseph Semprevivo, NGai Williams, Hernando Sanchez

clubs. Lorraine and Vicki were class officers. Joseph Semprevivo was running for sophomore class president and wore a T-shirt to announce the fact. It was the idle "cowboys," as they called do-nothing students, who were unhappy and got into trouble.

The group also agreed that many people in Deming seemed to take an unusual interest in what other people were doing, whether or not it was any of their business.

"Deming should be renamed Rumor Town," Vicki Wilcox said. "If you wear a baggy shirt to school, they all say you're pregnant."

Deming first graders

"We Are Going to Have a Better Deming"

ONE feature of Deming that does not come through immediately is that its population is divided fairly evenly between Anglos and Hispanics. Since Deming is only thirty miles from the Mexican border and since Luna County was a part of Mexico until halfway through the last century, this ethnic split is to be expected. Most Mexican-American families in Deming have long been U.S. citizens; however, a significant number of Mexican aliens, legal "green card" agricultural workers, live in and around Deming part of the year, particularly during the fall chile harvest.

The reason the nearly fifty-fifty ethnic split is not readily apparent is that most of the stores and businesses are run by Anglos, most professional and business offices filled with them, and most ranches and farms owned by them. It was also clear to us that—while there does not seem to be ethnic tension or antagonism—the two groups mingle very little in social situations.

We talked to Valentin Bustamante about these matters. Mr. Bustamante has lived most of his life in Deming and Luna County. As a young man he worked on farms, and then in 1946 he went to work for the state highway department and worked there for thirty-seven years before retiring recently. Now he is a machinery salesman for a truck equipment company.

"Social divisions are not new in Deming," he said. "They started as soon as the railroad brought Mexican workers here in the last century. In the early days there was a Hispanic settlement across the tracks. Hispanic boys swam in a dirt tank on the east side of town while Anglos used the town swimming pool. That has changed now.

"Hispanics are the backbone of Luna County's work force and always have been, but the money is controlled by the Anglos. There is some change in that, too. Thirty years ago there were almost no Hispanic businesses in Luna County; now there may be close to a

117

Mr. and Mrs. Bustamante and their son, Valentin, Jr.

hundred. Education is changing. Once only a few Hispanic teachers were in the school system, and they taught Spanish, nothing else. Now 40 percent of the teachers in the schools are Hispanic, and they teach all subjects."

Mr. Bustamante just managed to complete the seventh grade before he had to go to work full time, but he considers education one of the most important things in life. His years with the highway department were filled with training courses, seminars, and special workshops. He has a scrapbook entitled "Highlights in the Career of Valentin Bustamante," and it is full of awards of merit, certificates of appreciation, and exemplary performance citations.

"I am proud of my career," he said.

He is also proud of his children. The Bustamantes have three daughters; one has completed trade school, one has finished college,

Emma Armendariz with her sons, Jaime and Joel. Mrs. Armendariz teaches English at Deming High School, but both she and her husband are now studying for their doctorate degrees at the University of New Mexico. Speaking of ethnic divisions, Mrs. Armendariz says, "Deming is still really a polarized community."

and the other is a college senior in civil engineering. "And our youngest son—he is in the seventh grade—has just won a beautiful trophy in a mathematics competition in Las Cruces.

"When our children were born I told my wife that we would teach them English as their first language. They would start on an equal basis with other children. Education is a priority for most Hispanics now. We will do without anything—even food—in order to educate our children."

Mr. Bustamante has led an active public life, serving several times as president of St. Anne's Club, a large, mostly Hispanic organization within St. Anne's Catholic Church in Deming. A few years ago he ran for the office of county commissioner in Luna County. He did not win, but he has good feelings about the vigorous campaign he waged.

"I'm a builder, not a destroyer," Mr. Bustamante said. "We are going to have a better Deming."

Evidence of the change that Mr. Bustamante talked about is not hard to find. Deming's present mayor, Sam Baca, is Hispanic; he comes from an old Luna County family and runs Deming's only funeral home. Hector Madrid, also from a long-time Deming Hispanic family, is principal of Deming High School. And husband and wife Luis and Fermina Montoya are two of the most popular young business people in town. Luis is manager and part owner of an automotive parts store, and Fermina has her own beauty shop, Fermina's Coiffures.

"There is ethnic harmony in Deming High School," Hector Madrid said to us, and from a number of visits to the school, we thought that the principal's assessment was on target.

In Deming and Luna County the gap between Anglo and Hispanic economic well-being is still wide and social interaction still sluggish, but the prospects for future improvement do not seem bleak.

"I Belong Here"

MANY towns in rural America are slowly dying, some not so slowly, but Deming is not one of them. Despite the hard times for ranching and farming, Deming's vitality, stemming from both new and traditional activities, is strong. The Deming Arts Council, now well into its second decade, is a good example. It is also a good illustration of how knowledgeable and experienced senior citizens, moving to Deming because of the sunny, dry climate and moderate cost of living, can make a contribution to the town.

Paul and Margot Hoylan

Paul and Margot Hoylan moved to Deming after he retired from the U.S. Foreign Service. Deming is a far cry from some of the other places the Hoylans have lived—London, Paris—but, Mrs. Hoylan told us, "We came to Deming because in our last assignment, which was Stockholm, we never saw the sun."

Margot Hoylan, together with Marianne DeMott and Dorothy Tuma, founded the Deming Arts Council and served as its president for eleven years. Today it is no exaggeration to say that Deming has one of the most active cultural programs in the country for a town of its size. The Council has 165 individual and corporate members and a small but attractive Center for the Arts where exhibition of paintings, photographs, and textiles are held. Art instruction is provided for both children and adults.

Fermina and Luis Montoya with their daughter, Claudia Elena. Luis was named Chief Quacker for the 1987 Great American Duck Race. Despite the funny title, the job is a big one that is given only to trusted community leaders. It calls for months of planning and decision-making.

Kit Tremaine, a vigorous eighty-year-old who divides her time between Santa Barbara, California, and Deming. A philanthropist whose Sunflower Foundation gives away $2 million a year to social causes, Mrs. Tremaine has bought a building for the Center for the Arts. It will be used for instruction in ceramics, weaving, and other arts and crafts.

Kathleen Tijerina

Tom Hay, a retired university professor, and his wife, Kathleen Tijerina, moved to Deming from Albuquerque because of Albuquerque's size and high cost of living. A professional artist, Kathleen says, "I didn't have a studio in Albuquerque because I couldn't afford one. In Deming we spent $27,000 on a duplex, half of which has become my studio." Tom is currently president of the Deming Arts Council. Kathleen is director of the Center for the Arts.

In addition to sponsoring special activities such as a summer Arts in the Park program for children and an art exhibit to emphasize Luna County's rich Hispanic heritage, the Council brings in musical and dramatic programs from other cities; the New Mexico Symphony Orchestra and the Albuquerque Light Opera Company have both performed in Deming in recent months.

Deming has some special event almost every month, but, in addition to Butterfield Trail Days, two of the most special are the Great American Duck Race in August and the Klobase Festival in October. The Klobase Festival, sponsored by Deming's Czech community, was first held in 1928 and is one of the town's oldest traditions. It is truly an occasion for feasting and good fellowship. At the 59th annual festival in 1987, 3,200 pounds of barbequed beef and 2,400 pounds of Klobase sausage were served, together with huge amounts of coleslaw, pinto beans, rolls, and homemade pies and cakes. Over 3,200 people took part in the festival.

In 1980 a group of Deming businessmen, looking for a way to put some fun into the long, hot summer, organized a duck race, complete with a best-dressed duck contest, a Saturday night Duck Ball, and a Chief Quacker to organize the events. Out of that casual beginning has come the Great American Duck Race, three days of fun and nonsense, held every August. From forty to fifty thousand visitors now pour into Deming for the long weekend of races and festivities; national television has begun to focus on the event, and in 1987 the *Wall Street Journal* ran a front-page feature story about it. Duck owners from New Mexico, Texas, and Arizona make up most of the race entrants, but some come from as far away as Kansas, North Carolina, and Washington.

Some Deming residents are becoming concerned about the huge popularity of the three-day celebration. "It was supposed to be a way for Deming folks to have some fun in the summer," one merchant said to me. "No one ever thought it would become a national media event."

But every year the Great American Duck Race gets bigger, and the end does not seem anywhere in sight.

Robert Duck (his real name!) shown here with his 1987 winner. Mr. Duck lives in Bosque Farms, New Mexico. His ducks have won six times in the eight years that the Great American Duck Race has now been held.

FAR from dying, Deming actually has had some population growth in recent years because of the movement of older Americans to the southwestern sunbelt. But the appeal of Deming and its desert-mountain environs is not limited to senior citizens and retired people. Artists, people who can start their own businesses, and those who are willing to work for less in order to live in this special setting are attracted to Deming.

One of those is Bill McKinley. A few years ago Bill came to Deming to visit relatives. At that time he was a member of the Washington, D.C., police department and, over an eight-year period, had worked his way up from rookie cop to the position of special investigator. But he liked what he saw in Deming and made a bold decision.

Bill McKinley

Bill resigned from the Washington police, brought his family to Deming, and settled into a new way of life. Using skills developed earlier in doing designs and layouts for the National Aeronautics and Space Administration (NASA), he now runs the Mirage Gallery and is Deming's only commercial artist; his wife, Terry, has become the town's only travel agent.

"I wanted to raise my kids here, not back there," Bill told us. "They love it, too. My little guy is always talking about rabbit hunting."

Bill raises a hand a few inches over his head. "In the summer the stars are about this far above you. There's no pollution here. The air is absolutely clean. And the water! I'm a water drinker. My well is absolutely the best."

Samantha Feehan's story is not so different. Before coming to Deming in 1982 with her daughters, Heather and Stefanee, Samantha—everyone calls her Sam—lived in Pennsylvania, where she had a dress shop. At the time of their move, Heather was eleven, Stefanee nine.

"We—my daughters and a friend—found a piece of land a few miles out of Deming," Sam told us. "We sold everything we had except for a few bare essentials and bought the land and an old school bus. We lived in the bus while we made adobe bricks and built our house. The first evening a dust devil took off the canvas awning we stretched outside the bus. It was a quick lesson in the ways of the desert. It took us a year to build the house. It's a free-form house, I'm afraid. It's whale-shaped. It just sort of happened, not at all like our drawings.

"I have a growing appreciation of what we have, which isn't a great deal. There is a peacefulness in our house which just oozes from the walls. Living here has its problems; cows break into our garden, the well goes dry. There have been times when the problems were almost too much."

Sam has opened Sew What, a lovely little shop on Pine Street in Deming, where she makes dresses. "This country is not for everyone," she said. "Since we've been here, people have come and gone.

Samantha Feehan in her dress shop

But there has never been a time that I wanted to return to Pennsylvania. Now I feel as though I belong here."

It is hard country, this little corner of the American Southwest called Luna County. As Samantha Feehan said, it isn't for everyone; some people come, take a look, and head back to where they came from. They don't stay nearly long enough to wear out a pair of boots, which, according to Smokey Nunn, is the amount of time it takes for this desert-mountain country to get in your blood. Most people whizzing through on Interstate 10 must wonder why anyone would want to live in this place.

We have tried to answer that question by letting people like Joe Bill Nunn, Frank Smyer, Diana Milligan, and Bill McKinley speak for themselves and for a lot of people like them. There was another person who has a deep feeling for the land and who put his feeling into words with quiet beauty. He was a pig farmer, and he didn't want Paul to take his picture. Pig farmers, I concluded, are sensitive because people complain about the smell, especially when the wind blows hard toward Deming. But he was a happy man.

"This is the kind of life I like," he said. "I've got a nice house, a horse, a few chickens. I used a backhoe to clear a little land around the house, but the rest I left just like it was. I love the desert. I've got quail in my yard. Coyotes come and drink out of my swimming pool. I've killed rattlers on my doorstep—that's a little too much nature, maybe—and I've seen eagles sitting on the telephone pole out front."

And then he said again, "I just love the desert."

BIBLIOGRAPHY

Borderbelles Bicentennial Brand History. Borderbelles Organization of Grant, Hidalgo, and Luna counties, N. M., 1976.

Cameron, Sheila MacNiven. *The Best from New Mexico Kitchens.* Santa Fe, N. M.: *New Mexico Magazine,* 1978.

Clemons, Russell E., Paige W. Christiansen, H. L. James. *Southwestern New Mexico.* Socorro, N. M.: New Mexico Bureau of Mines and Mineral Resources, 1980.

History of Luna County, New Mexico (Supplement One). Compiled by Virginia and George Pete Measday. Deming, N. M.: Luna County Historical Society, 1982.

LaPorta, Jean, ed. *The History of Luna County.* Deming, N. M.: Luna County Historical Society, 1978.

New Mexico Agricultural Statistics, 1985. Donald G. Gerhardt, Statistician in Charge. Las Cruces, N. M.: United States Department of Agriculture, New Mexico Agricultural Statistics Service, n. d.

New Mexico: A Guide to the Colorful State (WPA American Guide Series). New York: Hastings House, 1940.

Pearce, T. M., ed. *New Mexico Place Names: A Geographical Dictionary.* Albuquerque, N. M.: University of New Mexico Press, 1965.

Russell, Sharman Apt. "Cooke's Peak." *New Mexico Magazine,* March, 1988.

Ungnade, Herbert E. *Guide to the New Mexico Mountains.* Albuquerque, N. M.: University of New Mexico Press, 1972.

INDEX